# The hit was about to go down

Lumbering across the street, a head taller than those around him, was a copper-skinned giant with long black hair. He wore a thin denim jacket over a faded work shirt, and torn jeans. A derelict—the perfect cover.

The two Forca Militar operatives in front of the hit man stopped dead, forming a barricade Bolan wouldn't be able to pass. The killer fell into step behind them and reached into his jacket.

Two more men followed behind the warrior—blue-suited headbreakers. They slowed to Bolan's pace. When the timing was right, they would hold him, or push him forward into the man with the knife. It would take only a few seconds, and everyone would vanish while their victim slumped to the ground.

Five feet from the Executioner, the assassin showed the blade.

Bolan could see the man's strong square teeth shining, glistening in a deadly smile as his hand tightened around the dagger's hilt.

Mack Bolan looked into the man's eyes, and in them he saw death.

# MACK BOLAN.

## The Executioner

# DON PENDLETON'S
# THE EXECUTIONER®
## FEATURING MACK BOLAN®

## FORCE DOWN

A GOLD EAGLE BOOK FROM
# WORLDWIDE.

TORONTO • NEW YORK • LONDON
AMSTERDAM • PARIS • SYDNEY • HAMBURG
STOCKHOLM • ATHENS • TOKYO • MILAN
MADRID • WARSAW • BUDAPEST • AUCKLAND

ISBN 0-373-61180-3

Special thanks and acknowledgment to
Rich Rainey for his contribution to this work.

FORCE DOWN

Copyright © 1993 by Worldwide Library.

Printed in U.S.A.

Those who have been once intoxicated with power...can never willingly abandon it.
—Edmund Burke
1729–1797

The powerful who prey upon the weak and innocent deserve no quarter—and they won't find any.
—Mack Bolan

# THE
# MACK BOLAN®
## LEGEND

Nothing less than a war could have fashioned the destiny of the man called Mack Bolan. Bolan earned the Executioner title in the jungle hell of Vietnam.

But this soldier also wore another name—Sergeant Mercy. He was so tagged because of the compassion he showed to wounded comrades-in-arms and Vietnamese civilians.

Mack Bolan's second tour of duty ended prematurely when he was given emergency leave to return home and bury his family, victims of the Mob. Then he declared a one-man war against the Mafia.

He confronted the Families head-on from coast to coast, and soon a hope of victory began to appear. But Bolan had broken society's every rule. That same society started gunning for this elusive warrior—to no avail.

So Bolan was offered amnesty to work within the system against terrorism. This time, as an employee of Uncle Sam, Bolan became Colonel John Phoenix. With a command center at Stony Man Farm in Virginia, he and his new allies—Able Team and Phoenix Force—waged relentless war on a new adversary: the KGB.

But when his one true love, April Rose, died at the hands of the Soviet terror machine, Bolan severed all ties with Establishment authority.

Now, after a lengthy lone-wolf struggle and much soul-searching, the Executioner has agreed to enter an "arm's-length" alliance with his government once more, reserving the right to pursue personal missions in his Everlasting War.

**1**

Hissing waves surged up the stretch of beach that bordered the rain forest. Smooth gray rocks studded the damp ground closest to the trees, casting a handful of jagged shadows onto the sand.

At a spear point of forest jutting into the Atlantic, a cluster of palm trees shifted in the strong night breeze, razor-edged fronds rattling together and brushing the shoulders of the sentry who stood on duty.

Unkempt black hair trailed down the collar of his jungle-colored camous. His right hand rested idly atop the barrel of the 9 mm submachine gun slung under his arm.

Despite the grim look on his face, this night he was taking up space more than he was standing guard. Now and then he looked with longing at the clearing that had been slashed out of the woods fifty yards inland, where camp fires burned brightly.

He listened to the laughter from the temporary camp, paying close attention to the one voice in particular. It was a high-pitched feminine voice that rode musically above the sound of bottles clinking together. It was the voice of their latest captive. Unfortunately she was one of the privileged ones. Nothing would happen to her. Until the ransom money was paid she was money in the bank for Forca Militar.

Her name was Clorinda Sertano and she was a privileged debutante from Rio de Janeiro whose life in the fast lane made her a legendary figure in the gossip columns. She was a one-woman soap opera with affairs from all levels of society.

Her father had sent her north to Belém, the bustling port city eighty miles upriver from the Atlantic, in the hope that running one of his subsidiaries would change her ways, teach her discipline and how to make her way in the world.

What a joke, the sentry thought. The woman had learned how to make her fortune, all right. The quickest way. Within one year of her arrival in Belém she had been cultivated by Forca Militar's underworld ambassador—cultivated, coopted and eventually controlled by the white powder the Ambassador sprinkled over her like magic dust. For a poor girl the coke habit would have been a problem, but not for Clorinda. She was offered an easy way out of her cocaine debts and a chance to make a fortune in the bargain.

All she had to do was let herself be kidnapped and leave the rest to the Forca Militar.

Images of the raven-haired woman danced through the sentry's thoughts as he lazily scanned the choppy Atlantic swells rushing in toward Marajó Bay. The sentry could afford to dwell on the baby-faced, full-figured hostage. He expected no trouble this night. There was little to fear. His job was to watch the water for the approach of the oceangoing yacht delivering the ransom. Arrangements had been made with Clorinda's company for her safe return.

It was a carefully choreographed operation. Forca Militar had done this several times before. When the yacht came in bearing the corporate bagmen, the FM team would move south to the rendezvous. If the money was there, the woman would be handed over to the rescuers. If not, she would be handed over to the men of Forca Militar.

And then she would no longer laugh, he thought.

A HUNDRED YARDS OUT to sea a black shape knifed through the water.

Completely clad in the colors of night, Mack Bolan swam just beneath the surface, breathing through long-duration shallow-depth scuba gear. The lightweight breathing apparatus was designed for special operations combat swimmers, providing up to three hours of diving time.

A SEAL unit had taken him halfway in to shore aboard a small four-man submersible SDV. The torpedo-shaped four-man swimmer delivery vehicle was designed to undetected insertion and extraction of special forces ops, delivery combat swimmers close enough to shore so that they weren't exhausted by the time they climbed up on land to start their mission.

At the halfway point, Bolan bailed out of the open-hatched SDV while it turned and headed back toward the submarine waiting for it out in open waters.

The lightweight scuba gear took him the rest of the way.

From here on in there was no official U.S. presence in the area. The U.S. had played its hand, he thought, an invisible hand throwing a wild card into the game.

Whatever happened onshore was completely up to Mack Bolan and the gods of fate and chance. Of course, chance had been helped along by a strong dose of reliable intelligence.

Bolan rode the waves toward shore, staying just under the surface of the water.

Nearing shore, he raised his head slightly above the surface to scan the target site off to his left. Moonlight splashed the white-foamed crests of the waves as he swam to the right and headed for a staggered rise of rocks that offered shelters.

He touched bottom, rolled forward with the lurching waves, then clambered up from the beach like a primordial creature from the sea ready to strike at its prey.

The warrior began to remove his gear, salt water running down his eyes and lips. The waterborne creature was gone, evolving second by second into another kind of night creature.

The Executioner had arrived.

THE PRISONER DRANK white wine, looking up through the tent's canopy of netting at the starlit night. She reached for the green bottle, but a thin but firm hand caught hers.

"No," Paolo said, prying her fingers off the neck of the bottle. "Enough courage for now. You must be presentable for the exchange. Drink all you want when you are back in the hands of your own people."

"Who says?"

"*We* say," he replied, gesturing at the rest of the tents pitched around the clearing. Some of the men were talking, some were looking their way. It was obvious what he meant. Clorinda Sertano was severely outnumbered and outmanned.

She glared at Paolo with coal-black merciless eyes. It was the glare of a woman long used to servants who would shrink from her gaze back in the city.

But the trick didn't work out here. They were too far from the city for such things to count. Paolo returned the stare, his dark eyes amused at her bravado.

"Come on, Paolo, relax with me a bit," she cajoled, leaning forward to reveal even more of her tanned cleavage from her unbuttoned sweat-soaked shirt. But he was immune to her charms. Just as he was immune to the whispers of his men with their coarse suggestions about how they could entertain themselves with the purebred beauty who was so obviously built for pleasure.

He ignored them all, despite their muttered misgivings about his manhood. But none of their complaints was ever said clear enough for him to hear.

Though Paolo was slight in stature, there was a quickness about him, a sureness in every movement that spoke of total confidence. Dangerous lights burned in his eyes whenever someone confronted him, light that illuminated the steady approach of death to those who didn't see things his way.

Though he was now a member of a rogue army, Paolo had real army training in his background. Unlike the others in the Forca Militar troop, he kept his hair cut short. He kept his wits about him, seldom drinking or smoking. Whenever he spoke it was matter-of-fact. And the fact was, people obeyed him.

The only person she'd ever seen him listen to with full respect was the Ambassador. Unfortunately Antonio Moura wasn't here to put him in his place. He was away creating more opportunities for Forca Militar. So it was up to her.

"One more drink," she said. "Or I'll report your insolence to the Ambassador."

He smiled, tracing his well-trimmed, freshly razored mustache. "By all means report me," he replied. "It will enhance my position with him. There is protocol to be followed, even here in the jungle. Rules of conduct."

"Rules," she scoffed, sweeping her hair over her shoulder. "There are no rules with your type."

"Despite what you think, we are not all animals," he said. "How would it look if I delivered you to your father's bodyguards blind drunk? This is a matter of business. The name of Forca Militar must be respected."

She laughed loudly. "Killing, trafficking and kidnapping are not businesses. If not for me and my *real* businesses, you'd be in town somewhere rolling drunks."

"Perhaps," he said. "That too is a business. Fortunately my prospects have changed considerably since my early days."

Paolo came from the *favelas,* hillside shantytowns of tin and cardboard that sprouted up around Brazil's cities like wild fungus, nourished by misery, poverty, murder and every strain of narcotic known to man. He'd escaped by joining the military, his natural prowess taking him far. Until some superior officers scapegoated him for killings they'd committed, he'd been assured of a solid career. He was lucky to escape with his life, moving deep into the interior, into the realm of Forca Militar.

Paolo poured the wine onto the ground. "You are under my protection. You are under my law. Just wait. If all goes well, soon you'll be free."

She shook her head, pouting. Then she folded her arms around her knees and fell into silence.

This wasn't the picture Moura had painted for her. A quick, almost adventurous sojourn in the forest, then the easy money would come her way.

But instead she'd been carted from safehouse to safehouse, boat to boat, then finally to Marajó Island at the mouth of the Amazon River where the brown water rushed into the ocean.

The island itself was very easy to get lost in. The size of Denmark, much of it was uninhabited, uninhabitable. The land itself was constantly changing, carved and molded by the Amazon, the river thirty miles wide at times, as much as fifty miles wide as it neared the Atlantic.

Though there were some small towns on the island, plantations and riverside villages, to Clorinda the wide green expanse was the end of the world, populated by animals and insects and men with guns. Not at all what she was accustomed to. But there was a hint of paradise in the air. The money. Soon the ransom would be paid and half of it would be given to her. Then she would be delivered back to the promised land of skyscrapers and penthouses.

HE MOVED SLOWLY through the trees, reconning the guerrilla encampment. Bolan knew approximately how many men traveled with the Forca Militar unit, but approximate wasn't good enough. Unless he took a head count before he started taking heads, he could end up approximately dead.

With nearly every step he took, vines impeded his progress, snaking at his feet, looping around his neck. Around him were the sounds of nocturnal creatures skittering in the brush. Man-size fronds whispered softly as he brushed through them, crouching low to mask his silhouette.

After a half hour of silent creeping he managed to map out the paths the two sentries made on their rounds. He also tallied the number of green-clad guerrillas. There were eight in all, one head honcho with the captive, five spread out around the camp, and the two armed sentries.

The Executioner made his preparations with instinctive calm, subconsciously working out the geometry of death, then mentally rehearsing the attach over and over in his mind.

He had made an important discovery as he moved closer to the main camp, listening to the sometimes hushed, sometimes loud voices of the guerrillas. They spoke in a mixture of Spanish and Brazilian Portuguese, hinting that this unit of the underground army was international in scope. Bolan could get by in both languages, enough to know what the men were speaking about.

And they were speaking about a captive who wasn't a captive.

It *was* a scam, just as Brognola's contact had said. The contact, Colonel Joaquim Almeiros, was one of the few Brazilian covert operators the U.S. still trusted in matters dealing with Forca Militar. Almeiros had tipped them off to the possibility that the woman might be in on the scheme. After all, the kidnapping from the streets of Belém had been too smooth.

Like most scions and daughters of wealth, Clorinda was schooled in security matters. She knew the necessity of moving in random paths, working with bodyguards, watching out for attacks from thieves or kidnappers, the kind of men who swelled the ranks of the Forca Militar.

True, she could have been kidnapped by a well-organized crew, but her abduction was suspicious from the start. She'd eluded her own bodyguards and then, most unusual for such a pampered woman, she drove herself to the outskirts of Belém. A short time later several witnesses saw her abducted by a two-vehicle assault team. It was too easy, almost as if she'd had a date to keep with her kidnappers.

When the inevitable ransom demands were made, Joaquim Almeiros used his covert contacts to insert himself into the operation. He'd made himself a key player in the negotiations and was even now traveling with the ransom crew. Only Almeiros knew another operation was in the works to save Clorinda.

At the moment Clorinda didn't look much in need of saving. Not now, not while she coquettishly teased the man standing guard with her. No, Bolan thought, not standing guard. Baby-sitting was more like it.

He lost track of the number of times the "prisoner" laughed, the number of times she leaned forward, clutching at the shoulder of the man enthroned in stony silence beside her. He was bronze-skinned, trim, regal somehow. Even out here in the wilderness he was right at home.

And the woman was trying to make the best of her situation. There was no trace of fear in her voice or in her actions. Even the Stockholm Effect, where hostages identified with their captors in the hope they would all come out of it alive, couldn't account for the way the woman was behaving.

From his forest-shadowed observation point, Bolan could tell that it was all a game to her.

But it was a deadly game. The men who worked for Forca Militar had murderous pasts, murderous futures. Bolan had no qualms about moving against them. Beyond that, there was an even greater reason for carrying out the mission. Clorinda Sertano might be a bogus captive, but the Forca Militar had real hostages in their possession, Americans who had never returned from a joint U.S.-Brazilian operation against an FM outpost.

The Americans might be dead, but they still deserved a chance.

And now, moving slowly in the lush green darkness, was the man determined to give them that chance. Stage One of the recovery operation was about to begin.

## 2

The man was still looking for his ship to come in, Bolan thought after he quietly circled back toward the seaward sentry.

It would have been easy enough to take him out with a hushed shot from the silenced Beretta 93-R. But there was always the chance of discovery when the man fell. He could cry out, he could thrash around in the bush.

And then the army would be upon him.

No. It had to be this way.

The Executioner's steps were slow and deliberate as he moved, sounding like nothing more than a breeze of the night. He willed himself not to concentrate too hard on his stalking, aware that many a man could tell when someone was watching him.

When death was about, the primitive sense that kept man on top of the heap rose to the surface. He'd seen it too many times to discount the fact that in combat zones a man's sixth sense often kicked in.

The warrior was half a dozen steps away, splintered moonlight falling on him between the palm tree fronds above. That was the man's weakness. He liked this spot too much and kept coming back to it. This was the spot where he counted his crooked cash coming in.

But it was fool's gold now. This was the spot where he would pay the price for trafficking with murderers.

The sentry moved suddenly then, and Bolan froze, ready to adapt his attack.

But the sentry still wasn't aware of the Executioner. The man was more intent on a cloud of gnats that descended upon his neck for a feast. His right hand swept his floppy bush hat off his head to swat at the stinging insects.

And Bolan closed the gap.

By the time the sentry put his cap back on, his survival instinct kicked into gear. He started to turn, weapon up, but he never made it.

Bolan lunged, his left forearm swinging up and around and thudding into the man's trachea. At the same time he hammered his right forearm against the back of the sentry's head.

While the stunned guerrilla went rigid from the shock of the attack, Bolan's right hand swept the submachine gun out of his reach in a split second, then reapplied the stranglehold, right forearm pressing the back of the head, left forearm closing in a vise of rocklike muscle.

The stunned guerrilla clawed at Bolan's locked arms, but by then the carotid artery was already collapsing and the man's brain was cut off from its supply of blood. He tried to lever himself back, standing on his toes, but Bolan kicked him behind the knees, breaking the man's last fragile stance.

It was all over in a matter of seconds.

The man's last ship had come in, Bolan thought. A destroyer. The warrior eased him down to the ground where the gnats resumed their feast, then headed back into the forest toward the other sentry.

He moved easily, quickly, the lay of the land embedded in his brain from the earlier recon. He passed by the string of Claymores he'd wired together on the shore side of the camp, more for effect than damage. He'd speared the mines into the ground at the base of a small ridge, aiming the explosives toward the strip of shoreward forest, running the wire to the hand-held firing device close to the camp.

The people in the camp wouldn't be hit—after all, he wanted the woman alive—but they would think they were under attack and would be facing the wrong direction when the real attack came.

He closed in on the other sentry, who at first appearance seemed to be more on guard, dutifully patrolling the strip of forest on the inland perimeter. But the man had fallen into a trancelike state, seeing but not seeing, walking in a self-induced hypnotic rhythm.

He wasn't aware of his surroundings at all—until Bolan's hammer fist thudded into the back of his skull. To keep him from crying out, the Executioner's left hand had forced the man's teeth together at the same time with palm-heel strike. His strangled choke was swallowed by the sound of the forest as he fell into eternal sleep.

Now the Executioner moved toward the camp itself. He reached the web of thick vines he'd wrapped the wire around, then depressed the handle of the firing device.

Fiery explosions whumped into the brush close to the shore like an artillery attack, jolting the men in the camp to their feet. They ran toward the edge of the camp that faced the water, looking for their enemy.

By then he was already in their midst.

Two of the guerrillas sprayed the forest with a lead fusillade, unleashing streams of automatic fire that burned through the shadows.

They turned at the last moment when they saw Bolan approaching them from the side. Like a doomed duet, both men swung their smoking submachine-gun barrels toward the warrior. At that moment, Bolan opened up with two bursts from the silenced Beretta, pressing the extended wire stock against his shoulder.

The dead-on 9 mm sweep knocked both guerrillas off their feet, casting them into the dark green brush.

With a shadowy movement, the Executioner leaped over an ember-filled camp fire. He came down hard, crouching instinctively as a burst of automatic fire ripped the air above his previous position. He caught his balance, zeroed in on the flame-spitting target, then stitched the gunner from chest to skull, dropping him back into the tent he'd clambered from.

There were five down and three to go when he tossed the stun grenade at the prisoner's tent, turning the section of forest inside out with white fireworks.

The woman screamed, the men cursed and the Executioner went to work, picking out one more guerrilla who was making a break for the forest. He chopped him from the side, the bullets hurtling the man into the brush with a loud crash.

An automatic pistol fired several wild shots, burrowing into the ground at Bolan's feet, then digging into the bark of the trees surrounding the camp. The Executioner drifted back into the forest wall of shadows and slapped a fresh magazine into the Beretta as the gunman continued firing blindly in his panic.

Finally the gunman settled on a target he *could* hit. "Kill the woman," he shouted. "She cut our throats, kill her...."

Only two men left, Bolan thought.

Both of the remaining guerrillas were closing in on the woman, the reason all of them were fencing with death's shadow in the middle of an Amazon island. Bolan also converged on the site, keeping close to the rim of shadows running along the trees.

He saw a heavyset man stampeding in front of the prisoner's tent just as the Forca Militar headman was leading her away toward the safety of the forest, pushing her in front of him. They would have made it, too, if not for the hysterical guerrilla waving his pistol at the woman's face.

"She brought them on us!" he shouted. "We're all dead, all dying because of her."

The headman raised his arm, palm out in a halting motion, recognizing the danger he now faced from his own man.

But the gesture had little effect.

"Kill her," the gunman repeated, still raging out of control. "Kill the bitch, or I will."

"No," the other man said calmly, slowly easing the woman away from her would-be assassin. But the voice of command no longer registered with the Forca Militar gunner.

He wanted to kill somebody, to strike out at some convenient enemy if he couldn't get the real one who'd dropped his companions with lethal accuracy. He was cracking under the strain of fighting a real soldier, not the usual civilian target of the Forca Militar.

"She dies—"

"Not yet," the headman stated, still aware of the need to evade the assassin who'd stalked their camp. He continued to pull the struggling woman toward the trees while trying to reestablish his authority. "Not until—"

But there was no "until." Even as he spoke, the leader of the Forca Militar unit brought his side arm from behind Clorinda Sertano's back, firing it just as it cleared her side. Two pulls of the trigger, two loud blasts, launched the guerrilla backward, a dark red hold blossoming on his shattered forehead.

Almost gallant, Bolan thought, how the man shielded the woman from harm. Except for one thing. He was really protecting his investment and perhaps his own life, thinking the only way he could walk away from this was to go ahead with the ransom exchange. He'd stayed close to Clorinda, knowing any rescuers wouldn't risk firing anywhere near her. And perhaps the panicked guerrilla gunman had realized that deep down, only the headman had a ticket out.

Bolan shouted a warning as he appeared behind the only surviving hardman.

The man spun around, no fear on his face, no surprise, as if he'd been expecting this. But he was still unable to stop Bolan's rush. The Beretta was already spearing forward while the other man's gun hand had yet to rise to get Bolan in his sights.

The Executioner had his target dead center and fired a single round.

The blast tore into the headman's shoulder, generating a geyser of blood and causing the pistol to jump from his fingers. Although the force of the 9 mm slug staggered him backward, he managed to stay upright. His left hand managed to reach the knife sheathed in his belt scabbard.

Bolan continued his advance, gripping the Beretta with both hands while his right foot launched a front snap kick to the man's knifehand. The white-hot blast of pain ended any thought of further resistance. A follow-up punch to the jaw dropped the man unconscious to the ground.

In that brief span of time, the woman ran toward what she thought was the safe harbor of the forest. Bolan caught up to her with a few quick steps and grabbed her elbow. She ran a few more steps until her momentum swung her around in a half circle. At the end of the turn Bolan released his grip and let her tumble softly in the high grass, flat on her khaki-clad behind, strands of her black hair spreading out like a halo of night around her head.

Helen of Troy, Brazilian-style, Bolan thought. The face that launched a rescue ship. Angled cheeks, searing eyes, and a bountifully filled blouse. It was a wonder she was still in one piece traveling with this crew.

Her hands spread out on the ground for balance as she sat up sputtering, her eyes charged with a haughty fire, which was quickly doused when she saw the cold-eyed warrior studying her like he was fitting her for a casket.

"Who are you?" she demanded. "You can't do this to me."

"From the look of things," Bolan said, glancing back at the body-strewed encampment, "I can do anything I want. The question is, what do I want to do with you?"

For the first time she looked unsure, as if she realized she might not walk away from this unscathed.

"What side are you on?"

"Don't be upset," Bolan said, "but I'm on your side. You've just been rescued. Not that you needed it a whole hell of a lot. If you ask me, Forca Militar needed rescuing from Clorinda Sertano.''

''Forca Militar?''

''Don't tell me,'' Bolan said. ''You never heard of them.''

''The kidnappers kept me in the dark—''

Bolan laughed. It was a harsh bark that cut to the quick. ''No games, Clorinda. Unless you're ready to play with your life.''

''What do you mean?'' she said.

''I mean unless you talk—I walk.''

''How will I get back home?''

''My guess is you won't make it.''

She started to stand up, but Bolan froze her in place with a sharp command. ''Not yet,'' he said. ''Stay put until I get a chance to debrief you. And believe me, it won't be the way you're accustomed to.''

While she kept a wary eye on her new captor, Bolan made a quick recon of the encampment. Seven dead, one wounded. He bandaged the unconscious man's shoulder, then looped a nylon cord around his hands. Not that he expected an attack from someone with his injuries, but the man had already shown his mettle once. No sense in taking chances.

He continued his search and discovered enough rations to last another week or two in the jungle encampment. Enough ammunition to fight a small war. Against farmers and Indians, maybe they would have won it, he thought. All this firepower was just for one cell. He tried to imagine the damage the whole network of Forca Militar could do with the right leadership.

It was a disturbing thought. A new kind of war was in the making, war for hire, war that recruited soldiers from the desperate straits of the third world and shipped them out wherever they were needed. Forca Militar was a frontier army and the frontier was a no-man's-land of murder, drug trafficking and kidnapping.

And there were damned few men capable or willing to patrol that border, Bolan thought as he looked up at the sky, a canopy of blackness pierced by starlight. All around him the lush forest whispered and hissed with life. It should have been a paradise untouched by the foot soldiers of anarchy. Instead it was one more Eden under siege.

Now and then glancing back at the woman, Bolan carried out a closer scan of the encampment. He dug through the packs and wallets, looking for maps, documents, American currency, anything that would tie this group in with the U.S. covert team that had vanished upriver—vanished with the help of Brazilian security rogues, he thought.

The whole operation had been compromised from the beginning. Supposedly the U.S. team and its Brazilian counterparts were going to strike a Forca Militar outpost, one of several weapons depots run by the underground army.

From the intel Bolan was privy to so far, the underground army was stockpiling arms for some of their newer clients among the island states in the Caribbean Sea, which recently had more than their share of well-armed coup attempts.

There were plenty of reasons for the U.S. to move against the Forca Militar organization. It was obviously a growing threat to the stability of South America and, closer to home, the Caribbean. But at the moment, the main reason for Bolan's presence was the plight of the missing Americans.

There were no signs of them at first.

But then, from one of the flap pockets of the unconscious guerrilla, Bolan uncovered a folded handwritten map. The roughly drawn sketch showed four locations scattered across the island. One of them, apparently the encampment the Executioner just hit, was marked with several *x*s.

Farther south on the map was a splintery inlet in the shape of a quiver. Forests flanked the water on both sides. A perfect ambush site, it matched the rendezvous point where the yacht was supposed to hand over the ransom. Selected by the Forca Militar, every advantage was theirs. If the rescuers tried anything, they could have been hit from all sides. At the same time the guerrillas could easily retreat into the forest.

Two other points were marked on the map. One of them was farther inland alongside a stream and appeared to be a cache of some kind, maybe food stocks or an ammo dump.

The remaining site was on what looked like a small ridge near the northern side of the island. It, too, had several small *x*s on it, just like the first encampment.

Maybe that was where more hostages were being held, Bolan thought. But there was no way of knowing for sure. Not until the surviving guerrilla regained consciousness. From the look of things, it might be a while.

The warrior returned to the woman on the edge of the camp. The black-haired siren looked up at him as if she were the one in control, not him. Falling back on *her* survival skills, she affected a pose designed to bring a man to the melting point. She leaned forward with feline grace, her palms splaying out on the grass in front of her and her body language saying she was his for the taking.

Anywhere else it might have worked, but not here.

The coppery scent of the dead bodies ruined the ambience.

But she seemed not to care. Pampered all her life, the center of the universe, she hardly paid a thought to the men who were so impolite as to die in her presence.

"Well," she said. "What are we—"

"Quiet," Bolan snapped. He crouched opposite her and said, "I'm asking, you're talking. Got it?"

She tilted her head to one side, raising her eyebrows as if she were still thinking about it. "I haven't decided."

"I have. You get one chance only. The instant I think you're holding anything back, you're on your own."

"Not quite," she said, almost smiling at him. "It's all been arranged. The boat will come for me."

"Yeah," Bolan replied, "*if* I give the signal." He looked hard into her eyes. As far as he was concerned she was a killer and deserved no quarter.

She read his mind, and she talked.

Three flares arched above the Atlantic as the seventy-foot yacht neared the inlet.

Comet tails of blue, white and red streaked through the darkness, pulsing out over the water in the sequence that had been worked out behind the scenes by Hal Brognola, director of the Justice Department's Sensitive Operations Group, and the Brazilian commander of covert operations, Joaquim Almeiros.

Bolan lowered the flare gun, then moved back into the cover of the forest where he scanned the approaching ship through a small hand-held night-vision scope.

The gleaming silvery yacht belonged to Sertano Industries. It was one of a fleet used to entertain corporate clients and host soirees that made a splash in the society columns. This night it was outfitted much simpler than usual—no party lanterns strung around the deck, no music blaring, no carefree laughter echoing out over the rush of the waves.

The only extra passengers for this cruise were half a dozen armed men, all of them studying the shoreline as the yacht drifted into the narrow waterway.

Bolan's reception committee was dead quiet, the woman because of her fear, the prisoner because he'd lapsed back into unconsciousness after coming around long enough for a hurried interrogation.

When Paolo Nazare, the leader of the Forca Militar unit, had gone under again, Bolan didn't force the issue. Without a chance to recover from his wounds, the guerrilla would have died.

Bolan was satisfied with the brief interrogation. In his dazed and vulnerable state, the Forca Militar chieftain convinced him that American hostages *had* been kept at the other camp that was sketched on the map. But they were no longer there. As soon as the ransom demands were made, a separate team of guerrillas moved them off the island. The guerrillas didn't want to risk losing both sets of hostages in the slim chance that a rescue operation was launched.

The warrior wasn't surprised at the precautions the guerrillas took. Though many of Forca Militar's rank and file consisted of *marginals,* untrained freebooters who did whatever it took to survive, the upper-echelon guerrillas knew how to wage covert war—stay on the move, stay hidden and stay in control.

Clorinda had also come clean about her involvement in planning her own kidnapping. It helped matters that she thought Bolan was a stone-cold killer, especially when he hinted that life would be a lot easier for him if he just liquidated both her and Nazare.

However tenuous, the Executioner had links to the lost Americans.

And here came just the man he needed to unravel the rest of the links—Colonel Joaquim Almeiros. He was riding into shore on a small outboard that had been lowered from the yacht. Accompanying him were three security men whose rifle barrels protruded from the sides of the boat like fishing rods.

Bolan followed their progress through the scope as all four men jumped over the side, splashing waist-deep into the water and hauling the boat up the rocky shore.

Joaquim Almeiros left his men by the boat, then walked uphill toward the heavily treed sector that had been the flare's point of origin, shouting out the name of the American who'd been sent to Marajó Island—Mike Belasko. It was one of the completely back-stopped cover identities that Hal Brognola and the Feds in Wonderland maintained for the Executioner.

"Up here," Bolan called, stepping out from behind a thick tree trunk with huge curling roots that gripped the edge of the bank. He aimed a pinpoint flashlight beam at the Brazilian.

Almeiros paused and looked toward Bolan, his wet shoes sinking into the sandy incline. "We must meet as equals," he insisted.

"Agreed," he shouted back. "Send the boat back to Belém, with your bodyguards aboard. Then we'll be equal. Or you can come up here where your men won't have me in their sights."

"You are a careful man."

"And a live one," Bolan said. "Make your choice."

"Very well," Almeiros replied, continuing his climb. When he reached the peak of the sandy ridge, Bolan stepped in his path, the Beretta at his side.

"Mike Belasko?"

Bolan nodded. "And you are?"

"Colonel Joaquim Almeiros," the other man replied. "Project Talon."

The man was brown-skinned, and his hair was dark and a lot longer than the photo in the dossier the warrior had seen. Parted in the middle, slanting over his prominent forehead, the jet-black hair made him look part Indian, as if he were becoming one of the warriors he'd befriended deep in the interior of the Amazon. He had high, sharply angled cheekbones and eyes that mirrored a keen intelligence.

After the two men checked each other's covert credentials via key code words relating to the operation, Bolan gave him a quick briefing of the situation, then led the Brazilian a short distance through the forest.

There, leaning against a tree with closed eyes and a blood-soaked bandage, was the guerrilla leader. "This man needs medical attention," Bolan said.

"What he needs is another bullet," Almeiros replied, staring down at the hardman.

"Could be," Bolan said. "But from what I've seen, he's ready to deal."

"He has no choice."

"Neither do we," the warrior replied, "unless we get him to a doctor."

Almeiros nodded. Then he looked at Clorinda, who'd hung back in silence. "And her?"

"She needs a jail," Bolan said. "Clorinda Sertano was a key player in engineering the kidnapping. I'm sure she'll tell you more about it on the ride home. She's as guilty as hell, but knowing the kind of money the Sertanos can throw around, I think prosecution will be a nonevent."

"And it might be a mistake," Almeiros said, glancing at the woman. His face softened for the first time. "Now, cooperation, that is a different matter. No trials. No scandals. Just the truth, just a bit of help is all we ask."

"What if I don't cooperate?" she said.

"Then I'm afraid I'll have to demand cooperation, instead of asking for it." Almeiros drew his side arm and leveled the weapon. "After you," he said.

The woman stood, protesting, but still eager to leave the rain forest. She accompanied Bolan and the Brazilian commando leader down to the shoreline where Almeiros's men ferried them out to the yacht. His men set off in the outboard once again, carrying a stretcher back to shore for the wounded man.

Paolo Nazare would eventually be transported to a military hospital, or more likely a safehouse under Almeiros's control, where a doctor he trusted would treat the man. As soon as he was up to it, he would be debriefed more thoroughly. So would Clorinda Sertano. Then a long-range game plan would be worked out with Brazilian security.

But in the meantime, Almeiros and the Executioner went below deck to one of the cabins commandeered by the Brazilian to work out *their* game plan. It was a covert war council, a meeting that would never exist officially. Because some of Joaquim Almeiros's greatest enemies wore the same uniform.

STILL CLAD IN HIS combat gear, Mack Bolan sat in a plushly furnished cabin, watched over by the unblinking eyes of the baroque paintings lining the oak-trimmed walls.

Joaquim Almeiros had stepped out a few minutes earlier, summoned by one of his aides to the communications room.

Bolan took one last swallow, then slid his empty coffee cup across the top of the small fold-out table that was bolted to the side of the cabin. It was his second cup of strong black coffee since he came aboard. He sighed heavily and rubbed his hand across the back of his neck. He was tired, and frustrated at getting so close to the Americans only to find them gone. And the mission itself evoked mixed emotions. It was successful in one regard. By freeing the woman and derailing a Forca Militar operation, Bolan had established his credentials with his Brazilian counterparts.

But in another regard it was a failure. The best-case scenario had called for the Executioner to carry out a quick hit, an in-and-out foray on Marajó Island that would extract American hostages, not just a jaded playgirl. Now the Americans were more out of reach than ever before.

"I don't see why we should wait any longer," Bolan said, when Almeiros returned from the radio room. "Let's head upriver and track them down."

The Brazilian nodded as he sat across from Bolan. "I understand your thinking. In your situation I would feel exactly the same. But..."

There were too many *but*s and *if*s for Bolan's tastes. Within the next half hour they'd found little common ground.

According to the latest intelligence available to Almeiros, during the past few days some Americans had been spotted at several locations upriver, always in the company of Forca Militar personnel. The guerrillas' riverboat had docked at a number of small villages for fuel and food while they hopscotched their way toward Manaus, the port city nearly a thousand miles up the Amazon. This confirmed Paolo Nazare's statement that the other set of hostages had been moved out while the ransom exchange was under way.

"Then why are we killing time down here?" Bolan asked.

"Because it is another world up there," Almeiros replied. "Not your world. Not even my world. Not yet. If we move too soon, we can lose everything."

"I'll take my chances."

The Brazilian leaned forward, elbows on the table, fingertips brushing aside his hair and massaging his temples. "And you are willing to take us down with you. You should remember that you were sent here to assist us. And in all honesty, I didn't think you'd survive this first stage."

"But you were willing to take the chance."

Almeiros nodded. "Yes. But only on the insistence of your superior."

"Superior?" Bolan queried.

"Hal Brognola. When he suggested bringing you into the operation, I thought I owed it to him because of our mutual successes in the past."

Bolan smiled without mirth. "Hal and I go way back, but he's not my 'superior.' We have an understanding that works for both of us. Sometimes he calls on me, sometimes I call on him. When we see eye to eye on things, we work together."

"And when you don't?"

"Then we do our best to stay out of each other's way."

Almeiros sat back in his chair, clasping his hands together and narrowing his eyes while he studied Bolan like a judge about to pronounce sentence. "Then you are totally separate from the U.S. government. You answer to no one unless you choose to?"

"That's how it's played so far."

"It plays well, my friend," the Brazilian said. "Very well. It appears we work alike. Neither of us wants to suffer bureaucracy but sometimes we must. And there are times bureaucracy can be useful. It can provide things we need. But to be truly effective we must be able to play a free hand when the time comes."

"Yeah," Bolan said. "Like now."

"The time is *coming*. First comes the logistics. We must get everything in place."

"Things already are in their place," Bolan said. "From what I've heard, you've got everything you need at the Jaguar school in Manaus. You're attached to them."

"At times, yes." The Brazilian special forces colonel was well-known at the army's jungle warfare training center in Manaus. Those who survived the courses wore a jaguar patch marking them as members of an elite force of unconventional warriors. It was a fitting choice. Jaguars were rare and sleek creatures who stalked the night. They owned the jungle.

Almeiros went to the training center first as a student, later as an instructor. In between he'd distinguished himself in the secret wars against Brazil's insurgent armies that were always springing up deep in the lawless Amazon interiors. For the past few decades Brazil had quietly put down subversive and criminal rebellions all across the Amazon.

Forca Militar was the latest in an inglorious history, and perhaps the deadliest. It was the first subversive group to create its own underground government that mimicked legitimate government in its organization. It had influential backers, sophisticated ambassadors and an army to enforce its law. The law was very simple—survival of the fittest. Wealth belonged to those who could take it. It was a country always on the move, one without borders.

"Let me be perfectly frank with you . . ." Almeiros said.

The Executioner listened intently, matching those details he'd already known with the ones offered by the Brazilian counterinsurgency chief as he explained more about his background and the scope of his current operation.

He'd moved into Brazilian intelligence, specializing in internal security at stations in Rio de Janeiro, Brasília, Manaus, and several other postings throughout the country. Just recently he'd been called back into the special forces arena to deal with Forca Militar. At first there was a lot of opposition to placing him in charge of the field operations. But he won out because there were enough high-powered spooks backing him. It was a razor-edged victory. Some of the gray-haired intelligence chiefs were looking to stab him in the back at the first opportunity, and some of the army men—collaborators of Forca Militar—were literally looking to stab him in the back.

"You see," the Brazilian went on, "I, too, need men like you. Men who are untraceable to government operations, loyal only to me, and who can strike wherever they are needed. I need them to be willing to infiltrate Forca Militar and to put their lives on the line for me—as I do for them. Even now I am gathering them, moving them into position. Believe me, we *will* move against the guerrillas as soon as we are able. But if we move too soon, all is lost."

"Including the Americans?" Bolan asked.

"Perhaps. I would be lying to you if I said otherwise. You see, we don't even know for sure if the Americans seen with Forca Militar are prisoners. They could be renegade mercs, traffickers, dealers. There are a lot of American faces in the underworld. Then again, our intelligence might be faulty. Many of our underground contacts are not the most reliable. People who ask too many questions in the Forca Militar do not have the greatest life expectancy."

As the Brazilian counterinsurgent specialist outlined his operation, Bolan realized that he, too, was becoming one of the soldiers in Almeiros's war. If the Executioner was willing to risk his life for the cause, the man was willing to take him aboard. On his own terms and in his own time.

After covering more details about the capacity of his jungle troops as well as his civilian power brokers in the cities, Almeiros assured Bolan that even now a quiet but exhaustive search was underway on Marajó Island for the Americans. If they were there, they would be found.

"That's it, then," Bolan said, pacing around the small room to stretch his legs. After the wide open spaces of the forest it seemed claustrophobic and alien to be confined to the small quarters of the yacht. "We agree we have to move. We just don't agree on when. I don't mind telling you that I don't like the timetable. I like to keep in motion."

"Then I have some good news for you."

"Shoot," Bolan said.

"When I left you earlier," the Brazilian said, "it was because of an urgent message from our mutual friend."

"Brognola?"

"Yes. He needs you for an impending strike against another Forca Militar unit."

"Where?"

"I suspect somewhere in the Caribbean," Almeiros replied. "They've been carving out new territory. This group is like a hydra. There are many heads to chop."

"Why didn't you tell me earlier?" Bolan asked. "We should have made arrangements."

Almeiros shrugged. "Arrangements have been made. Even now we are heading for a rendezvous in deep water where you will be transferred to a U.S. warship. From there, I understand you will become a passenger on a noncommercial flight to a pre-arranged destination."

Bolan had noticed the increase in speed and the swaying of the oceangoing yacht as it plowed over the waves. Hal Brognola had told him beforehand than Marajó Island was just one of the beachheads in the war against Forca Militar. Time to move on?

"Mind if I confirm the arrangements with Brognola?" Bolan asked.

"By all means." Almeiros glanced at his watch. "Let's go. My radio operator should be making the connection even as we speak."

"Right," Bolan said, heading for the door. "You're pretty sure of yourself."

"I'm sure of one thing," the Brazilian replied as he led the way down the corridor.

"Yeah?"

"I'm sure that you will make it back here in one piece. And by then, my friend, we'll be ready to move."

"I'll put it on my calendar."

**4**

Antonio Moura stood on a small backwater dock spearing out into the dark brackish water of the Amazon tributary, sixty miles southwest of Manaus. The rickety dock reflected the jungle-shrouded settlement onshore, a place where lean-tos evolved into shacks, shacks into bars and bordellos, and bordellos into squalid hotels for underworld clientele.

When the time came to move on, the settlement would collapse just as quickly as it sprang up, and once again the jungle would blanket the area with a comfortable green darkness.

Moura liked operating in such shadows, in darkness ruled by the bloodred currents of violence pulsing through the interior of his brain, always moving, changing, carving out new territories in the name of Forca Militar.

The organization was an underground empire, and Moura was its ambassador.

He had a tanned bronze complexion, compliments of his Portuguese ancestors, and an aristocratic bearing that stemmed from an illusory kingdom in his mind. It was a kingdom he was always ready to defend. Moura had the build of a hangman more than a statesman. His broad shoulders, chest and his strong legs and rapid reflexes were like those of a swimmer, adrift in an underworld sea since his early teens.

Though he could easily remain in the relative safety of the city and conduct his business from there, Moura ventured into the wilds at every opportunity. Out here the law was a most elusive and unreliable denizen. Law was a creature made in his own image. A predator.

The men who now toiled on the riverbank behind him, rushing to and fro in the shadows of the lantern-lit dwellings, recognized that implicitly. They carried heavy crates of weaponry without a complaint, stacking them alongside the docks.

The crates contained machine guns, submachine guns, pistols, grenades, ammo, rocket launchers, all from Força Militar's underground depot. Some of the weapons were stolen from army bases, others made expressly for Força Militar on midnight manufacturing runs in factories coopted by the underground army.

In a short while a flotilla of riverboats would cruise down the tributary to pick up their cargo. This night's clients were old and valued customers, a cadre of gunrunners from neighboring Guyana and Suriname who would take the weapons of war back north with them. Their purchases had increased a great deal in recent years along with Força Militar's ability to supply them. It was a good business for men willing to take the risks. The high-quality weapons brought them great profits as they made their way into lawless hands.

The gunrunners operated almost as efficiently as Forca Militar, Moura thought. They dealt only with men they knew personally, which was one of the reasons why Moura was there to welcome them. Another was to pump them for information. The gunrunners had ambitions of their own. They wanted to branch out of their own countries and establish links with the Caribbean nations.

That ambition matched Moura's plans. Not only would he make a profit selling weaponry to the gunrunners, but they would also do some work for him. In order for Forca Militar to survive, it had to keep opening up new markets. The latest was the Caribbean where poverty, politics and unrest were creating a great demand for sophisticated weapons. It didn't matter who opened up the territories. Sooner or later Forca Militar would own them all, courtesy of Antonio Moura, Ambassador at large.

At the moment the Ambassador carried a three-inch steel blade sheathed inside his belt, its slender mass hidden by a brass buckle. He also had a compact Smith & Wesson 61 Escort single-action automatic holstered at the small of his back, easily hidden beneath his windbreaker. These were his diplomatic credentials.

The automatic was a gift from an American agent freshly deceased at the time the gift changed hands.

Antonio Moura smiled at the memory. It happened right there on the edge of the same dock where he now stood.

The American had come to Brazil with all the precautions of a wallet-bound tourist, arriving in broad daylight at their free-market paradise, a place where any kind of business could be conducted out in the open.

The American agent hadn't understood that.

In his guise as a Yankee trafficker in weapons and white gold, the undercover man had cruised up to the dock aboard a sleek powerboat staffed by Brazilian security operatives.

Like an explorer about to conquer a new frontier, the American had leaped onto the dock and walked straight up to Moura, certain that in a few moments he was going to make the world safe for democracy again. Bust all the bad guys and go home a conquering hero. The man was totally unaware that instead of backing him up, the security men were actually delivering him to the enemy.

Within seconds the Ambassador's retinue surrounded the agent, bright new gleaming submachine guns pointing at him like dowsing rods as they herded him toward the end of the dock.

Moura had strutted up to the American who by now had his hands raised in surrender.

Without warning, razor-sharp metal flashed in the air, an unsheathed explanation of the terms of surrender. The point of the blade stabbed into the agent's chest. A sharp tug did the damage.

Moura's knife hand snapped back in a blur, blood slicking the blade. He stepped back and nodded at his men, a signal for them to deliver the coup.

A sustained burst of automatic gunfire ripped through the darkness, streaming from the sleek new weapons wielded by the Forca Militar's guerrillas. The slugs chewed into the agent's body with 9 mm teeth, engaging him in a macabre dance of death before dumping his lifeless corpse onto the dock.

Moura glanced solemnly at the men who gathered around him in a half circle, wearing the satisfied smiles of fishermen who'd speared a good catch.

He shook his head in mock sadness. "Too bad he didn't understand *our* laws. The man thought he was in America."

Boisterous laughter floated above the water, a jeering send-off for the agent.

The corpse was removed then, making a dead splash before it was borne away by the river.

Only the Smith & Wesson stayed behind as a souvenir for the Ambassador.

The memory vanished as a wavering spotlight played upon the water. Moura's customers were arriving.

But there was only one light.

One boat.

And it was coming in fast, the whining engine sounding loud and clear in the stillness.

Moura shouted a warning and the shantytown lights were extinguished immediately. Half a dozen guerrillas took up positions around the docks while several others slipped into the riverbank shadows.

Then the spotlight flashed on and off in a sequence that marked it as belonging to one of Moura's men.

A few moments later a familiar voice called out his leader's name. It was Pedro Luna, one of Moura's "diplomats" from Manaus. Luna had graduated from police work to an intelligence posting until a slight matter of embezzled funds caused him to be expelled from the enforcement fraternity. Ripe for another kind of fraternity, Luna was recruited immediately, finding a well-deserved place in Forca Militar.

The boat cut its engines and knifed toward the dock. As it thumped against a splintery waterlogged post, Luna's wraithlike frame scrambled over the side.

While Moura's men tied the boat, Luna pulled the Ambassador out of earshot.

"What is it?" Moura asked, speaking softly and gesturing with a wave of his right hand for the newcomer to calm down. By all rights Pedro Luna should have been in Manaus counting money and courting underworld connections, not trekking down the river at breakneck speed. "What is the matter with you? Relax and tell me the problem."

Taking his boss's cue, Luna composed himself and explained that he had news of the prisoner exchange at Marajó. "There were problems," he said.

"No problem is too great," Moura responded, forcing himself to keep a bland expression on his face, as if he had been anticipating some trouble as a matter of course.

Luna hesitated for a moment. He was still nervous, clasping his hands together like a penitent about to make a confession. "Our people on Marajó were killed."

The Ambassador tilted his head slightly as if pondering the possibility. Then he shook his head in dismissal. "That can't be so. I've seen the Yankees themselves when they were brought to one of our camps. The prisoners are safe."

Luna nodded vigorously. "I'm not talking about the prisoners," he said. "*They* are safe. They made it off the island. But the woman—"

"Impossible," Moura said, picturing their comely accomplice. "I gave orders that she wasn't to be harmed. At least not now. She can be useful. No one would kill her."

"It's worse than that. The woman was rescued. All of our men were killed or taken captive."

Moura stood perfectly still as Luna filled him in on the destruction of the Forca Militar unit and the aborted ransom exchange. Though a part of his mind had always considered the possibility of a rescue attempt, it was mostly hypothetical. He had planned too well. The Sertano woman was in his pocket and so was the money of the Sertano family. Or so he thought. That had changed. Now he had to roll up some of his operations, the ones that could be exposed by talkative prisoners. He had no doubt that the Forca Militar men would talk. He knew from personal experience a man could be made to reveal anything.

He stood perfectly still and seemed totally composed. But the sparks that ignited in his eyes told a different story. They were the eyes of a seer. He was looking into the future, which was stained with blood.

Luna was familiar with that look and knew what it meant. Antonio Moura had just declared war.

## 5

Hal Brognola stood on the tarmac in a dark blue windbreaker, watching the olive drab Sikorsky helicopter coming home to roost at the Air Force base.

In the bright glare of the southern sun, Brognola looked almost trim again, the close-fitting custom jacket seeming to erase the bulk that had accumulated during his years spent behind a desk in Washington, hatching covert operations that had silent echoes the world over.

Despite the years of bureaucratic battling that had turned his hair gray and given him more stabs in the back than he could count, Brognola thrived on working behind the scenes. It seemed as though a magnet drew the old war-horse back toward the front lines.

A cloud of grit and dust billowed across the tarmac as the Sikorsky Black Hawk touched down. A few moments later the man most often on the front lines for the Sensitive Operations Group appeared in the open cabin door of the chopper.

Mack Bolan waved casually to the pilot, then jumped to the ground, carrying his gear in his left hand.

The chopper crew knew the man in black only as a nameless government op they'd ferried from the deck of a Navy warship off the Florida coast. To them Bolan was another John Smith whose line of work could very quickly turn him into a John Doe. Bolan had the eyes and the gait of a military man. Uniforms weren't required to know what he was about. One way or the other, it was obvious he was bred for war.

As he headed for the one-man greeting party, the Executioner noticed a helicopter crew readying another Black Hawk for a mission. Painted black for night flights, the chopper was equipped with the latest in electronic tracking and navigating equipment.

Beyond the chopper was a row of unmarked Piper Cheyennes and Cessna Citations, the high-tech trackers that U.S. customs used as part of *their* air force. The customs unit was an elite force of handpicked, highly trained officers who carried a variety of Heckler & Koch submachine guns, 9 mm automatics, shotguns and short-barreled .357s that hid a lot of stopping power in their small holsters.

The air base was just a hop, skip and a bust away from the Everglades, and a stone's throw south of Miami, both havens for traffickers of every stripe. The customs commandos operating from the base had racked up a hell of a score against drug and gun smugglers who considered Florida a giant lottery where they either got busted or made a fortune.

The fact that Bolan had been ferried to Florida clued him in that Brognola was gearing up to launch a Caribbean operation, just as Joaquim Almeiros, their man in Brazil, had said. Then again, Bolan had enough experience with Brognola to know that this could all be a smoke screen for the real mission— running down terrorists in the arctic.

His last briefing with Brognola had taken place in a subbasement office complex in Washington, D.C., one of several underground rabbit warrens maintained by the government—and one of the reasons it was known in the covert community as Wonderland.

Back then Brognola was wrapping up another clandestine campaign, though he'd known at the time that Forca Militar was looming on the horizon and had to be dealt with.

"Glad to see you made it back," Brognola said, taking Bolan's hand in a sturdy grip.

"Yeah, I managed to come out of it in one piece. Though I think we left a lot undone down there."

"Me, too. That's why I'm sending you back there as soon as Joaquim's Jaguars are ready. In the meantime you win an all-expenses-paid trip to the Caribbean."

"Don't tell me," Bolan said. "Courtesy of Uncle Sam."

"Jackpot. I'll tell you all about it in there." He pointed toward the steel-braced glass entrance of a long whitewashed building that looked like a prefab motel.

They walked past a group of customs personnel who paid little attention to either of the two men. They were used to all manner of government spooks haunting their territory.

ICE-COLD AIR BLEW across the shrunken islands of the Caribbean—the ice was in the air-conditioning, and the islands were drawn-to-scale graphics projected onto a screen in a briefing room at the base.

Stretching like a horn of plenty, the Caribbean islands wound from the northeast coast of South America up to Florida. Beginning with Trinidad and Tobago, there were about thirty islands laid out in stepping-stone fashion. Grenada, Barbados, Saint Lucia, Montserrat, Haiti, Jamaica and several other tropical nations curved up toward the Bahamas, then on to Florida.

One paradise led to another, or more accurately, one "paradise lost" led to another. As deadly as the hurricanes of August and September, poverty and crime hit the islands full-force, just as randomly, and seemingly just as unstoppable.

Sudden gusts of violence weren't uncommon even in upscale tourist towns when heavily armed criminals went on shooting and shopping sprees. Sometimes the violence ignited sporadic looting, which in turn caused iron grates to sprout up like weeds in front of store windows.

In this desperate atmosphere, drug and arms traffickers flourished, bringing with them an underworld apparatus for conducting business.

There were some victories.

Sometimes the crime waves would break just as suddenly as they began. Many of the perpetrators moved on or wiped each other out in urban ambushes. More rarely they were caught by the police and security agencies forced to play a catch-up game with them.

But inevitably, after the lull, another island would fall under siege as a new killing season swept in. These deadly storms once again appeared out of nowhere with few forecasters able to pinpoint the trouble.

But now, standing at the head of the briefing room like a gun-toting weatherman, Hal Brognola was doing his best to identify the hot spots.

He pointed to an electric-blue-and-green map of the Caribbean splashed on the screen to his right. Using a wand-thin laser pointer that danced a bright white pinpoint of light across the screen, he traced the trail of violence.

As the light beam skipped from island harbors and resorts to clandestine airstrips carved out of the jungle, Brognola recited a litany of busts, shootouts and escapes made by the "incoming" as he referred to the traffickers who were just as deadly as missiles raining on the U.S.

Some of it was familiar territory to Mack Bolan, as it was to many of the men gathered in the room, mostly blue-shirted customs and Coast Guard officers along with the plainclothes DEA operatives. Most of them had been in on some of the bigger busts and lesser-known firefights in the war against traffickers.

But as the coordinator of interagency strikes, Brognola wanted to make sure all the units shared the same intelligence.

It was a "getting acquainted" session so that farther down the road these same men wouldn't be getting killed by their own kind.

With the soft-touch remote control unit, the big Fed paraded a series of images on the screen. Surveillance shots from customs aircraft showed just about every type of plane and go-fast boat used by the traffickers. The planes captured them on film, radio and radar, and passed the intel to the Black Hawk pursuit choppers and Blue Thunder twin-Mercury speedboat interceptors used by customs. Customs and the Coast Guard often worked together on joint operations against the incoming traffickers. Though there were a lot of victories, the flow always continued.

"For some time now it's seemed almost as if we were facing an army of traffickers," Brognola said. "Unfortunately, gentlemen, the time has come to do away with the word 'almost.' There's a real army out there deploying troops from Brazil right up to the Bahamas. Initially the troops were isolated bands of enforcers working for the drug gangs. But now they've become organized. They're disciplined, powerful and have almost unlimited potential."

Some of the men nodded as Brognola spoke. Intuitively they'd known there was an organized force out there, one that could send in reinforcements just as quickly as a real modern army could.

"It's called Forca Militar," Brognola continued. "Also known as the Amazon Army. Their headquarters are in Brazil's major cities—Brasília, Rio de Janeiro, São Paulo, Belém and Manaus—but they also operate from bases in the Amazon where they've established a burgeoning trade in high-grade weapons. Those weapons have begun showing up in the Caribbean."

Brognola flashed several more slides on the screen, showing different types of weapons confiscated from groups supplied by Forca Militar. The weapons slides were replaced by high rises and luxury villas whose purchase was made possible by their profits.

"Like the Triads, the Mafia and the cocaine cartels, Forca Militar uses legitimate businesses as fronts to infiltrate and take over other corporate entities. But as the name implies, they are also a military organization. In recent months they've openly challenged the authorities, flaunting their power by co-opting or killing Brazilian special forces that have gone after them."

Brognola ran though another sequence of slides. A host of Brazilian faces appeared on-screen, one after the other, faces of the dead—police officers, judges, intelligence agents, soldiers. Then five more faces appeared on-screen, those of the American covert team believed dead or missing. "And we lost some of our own on a joint operation with a Brazilian counterinsurgency unit," the big Fed added.

He kept the camou-streaked faces on the screen, ensuring that they were branded into the memory of the exclusive audience. "So far there've been few signs of our people," he said, "or the Brazilians who went in with them. It's like they vanished off the face of the earth. What little we know is mainly bad news.

"Shortly after the agents vanished, a number of other American operations in the region were blown. Logic dictates that members of our strike team were captured and interrogated, subsequently exposing other U.S. assets. We don't know if they're still alive and undergoing further interrogation or if they've been killed. They could also be held for ransom, another Forca Militar specialty.

One reason we don't know what happened is that the highest levels of the Brazilian government have enforced an information blackout, the rationale being that anti-American sentiment could reach dangerous levels if word gets out about involvement of U.S. military personnel. Since many sections of Brazil *are* ripe for rebellion, this isn't just a smoke screen. Although it is a damn convenient way to cover up any links to Forca Militar."

A pilot with a weathered face and a growling scowl leaned forward in his chair. "Does this mean we're supposed to forget our boys down there? Sounds like the same kind of nightmare we went through after Nam."

Brognola shook his head. "This is one case where history won't repeat itself. That's why we're all here today to coordinate our activities. Many of you will be striking back at Forca Militar in the Caribbean. After we turn the heat on them in the islands, some of you will help to prepare a strike at the heart of the Amazon where we believe our men are being kept."

The mood in the room changed then. Rather than sit back and do nothing while MIAs suffered, this time they were going to act.

Some of what went down would be strictly according to the rule books. But not a man in the room doubted that another part of the operation would be totally off the books.

Brognola flashed a blank slide on the projection screen, then stepped to the front of the room. "Hard intelligence on Forca Militar is still coming in from those sources in Brazil who still have our trust. At the same time we're unraveling disinformation fed to us by Brazilian officials collaborating with Forca Militar or at the very least looking the other way. That's why they've gotten so strong so quickly.

"Make no mistake," the big Fed continued. "This underground army is heading for our shores, step by step, starting with the Caribbean. Unless we stop them now it'll be an underworld occupation army, almost impossible to remove."

He stepped to the side and flashed a new slide on the projection screen, showing the island of Jamaica. The laser pointer blazed over the dark green island like a small sun.

"This is where the operation begins," Brognola said. "Jamaica is the latest target of Forca Militar. They're trying to establish a major presence on the island."

"Are they working with the posses?" asked a black DEA agent who sat off to one side, his massive forearms folded across his chest. Bolan recognized him from a past operation he and Brognola had been involved with. His name was Jacques. He was also Henri, William, Francis. Depending on the situation, he had several identities to call upon. And from what Bolan recalled, Jacques spoke nearly as many languages as he had names.

Brognola shrugged. "In a way they'll deal with the posses," he said, a tired smile appearing on his face. "Their way. Initially they have to deal with underworld locals. But eventually they'll take over the entire operation. Naturally they'll keep some Jamaicans on board as figureheads, but in reality Forca Militar will call all the shots."

The head Fed chomped on his unlighted cigar, then said, "Except for the ones we fire."

**6**

The airbus from Miami landed at Montego Bay at two o'clock in the afternoon.

Bolan stood in the aisle to stretch his tall frame, then drifted along with the disembarking passengers— mostly middle- and upper-class Jamaicans returning from the U.S., or English and American tourists coming to Jamaica for a Caribbean retreat.

Traveling under the alias Michael Belasko, Bolan was here as a tourist. At least for the moment. No weapons. No combat gear. No official ID.

Humid air enveloped him on the way down the steps, making him feel about ten pounds heavier for several moments, the air-conditioning of the plane quickly fading into a cool memory as he joined the throng heading for the terminal.

It didn't take long to grow accustomed to the climate again. The tropical heat made life a bit slower and people more patient, conserving their energy for moments that mattered.

Inside the terminal a group of Jamaican acrobats and singers, part of a festival, were using up more than their quota of energy for the day as they performed for the long line of tourists. Caribbean rhythms of reggae and soca echoed throughout the high-walled receiving area, as security men and customs officials processed the incoming crowd.

After a wait of ten minutes Bolan showed his papers and "vacation itinerary" at one of the first checkpoints, then moved on to an exchange booth where he converted some currency, getting about six Jamaican dollars for each American.

He walked down a flight of stairs, picked up his luggage from the revolving platform, then passed through customs without a second look.

He headed through a cavernous hallway filled with booths from the tour companies, offering bus and limousine rides to the resorts and towns along the coast where about a hundred and fifty people were making their connections.

A well-dressed Jamaican in his twenties singled Bolan out of the crowd and drifted through the tourists toward him. "Anywhere on the island, mon," he said as he approached Bolan. "Right price, right driver." He gestured through the concourse window at a huge lot full of row upon row of tour buses and limousines.

The limos were mostly a decade or older boatlike Buicks or Chevys in perfect condition. Pointing toward a long Chevy with gleaming chrome and a fresh coat of lime-green house paint, the would-be driver reached out for Bolan's suitcase and said, "Hey, mon, let's get you started on slowing down." He spoke with the easy charm and confidence Bolan often encountered in the Jamaican people.

"Thanks," the Executioner said. "But I've got other arrangements."

"No problem." Then with a conspiratorial nod, the man leaned forward. "Next time, though, you ask for me, Eddy Lee, best driver this side of the island."

"You got a deal."

As Eddy Lee moved on to another incoming tourist, a deep basso laugh sounded behind Bolan.

The warrior turned and saw a familiar face sporting an impeccably groomed beard from cheek to cheek, blending in with his close-cropped hair.

"*Very* good decision, Mike," Sydney Beckett said. "Eddy's a good driver. Too good. He can turn a ten-mile drive into a three-day excursion just like that." He snapped his fingers.

"I wouldn't mind getting lost for three days now and then."

"Yeah," Beckett replied, "you came to the right place for that. But first we must do some business. The, uh, merchants from Brazil are carving out some new markets. And I do mean carving."

"That's why I'm here."

"You are most welcome. Especially under these circumstances."

U.S. and Jamaican security worked closely these days as a natural outgrowth of their increasing economic ties. Nearly fifty percent of Jamaica's legal trade was with the U.S. Then there was the illegal trade, the ganja express, which these days also moved cocaine and weaponry. The growing power of the traffickers brought the narcotics-enforcement agencies together. That led in turn to increasing intelligence-sharing and collaboration.

"Come on," Beckett said. "Everything's all set." The Jamaican security man led Bolan through the wide double doors into the parking lot.

Beneath the bright afternoon sun he moved with a casually precise walk. Even with the light blue cotton print shirt and jeans, Sydney Beckett carried himself like a military man.

Although his exact occupation wasn't known to the general public, Beckett was part of an elite unit that worked behind the scenes, smoothing the troubled waters that often rushed ashore on Jamaica.

Beckett was Jamaica's security liaison with the intra-Caribbean counterterrorist force that came into existence shortly after the Grenada coup. Known as the Caribbean Regional Security System, the bulk of the elite troops was provided by Jamaica and Barbados, and Beckett was usually at the head of those covert troops.

Currently he was working on the Jamaican end of the Forca Militar smuggling operation, concentrating on the suspected "end users" of the contraband.

He led the Executioner past a gauntlet of gleaming tour buses, ultramodern air-conditioned vehicles gradually filling with tourists, many of them drinking Red Stripe beer from vendors working the lot.

"Here we are," Beckett announced, walking to the side doors of a small bus that looked like a carbon copy of all the others. At least on the outside.

But inside it was different. There were only five passengers and a driver, all military-looking men who sat up front talking in subdued voices while reggae music played on the radio.

The back of the bus was filled with duffel bags, lockers and a weapons rack. The men glanced briefly at Bolan as he and the Jamaican security man moved toward the rearmost seats.

"Now," Beckett said softly, leaning back and stretching his arms over the cushions, "as to why we are here..."

As the bus rolled out, he briefed Bolan on the current temperament of Jamaica. Occasional outbreaks of violence still shook some of the crowded inner-city areas of Kingston and other towns, but overall the island had stabilized during the past few years.

The bus wound through the streets of Montego Bay, steadily moving uphill past the hotel complexes and out into the countryside where shacks and stilted windowless huts stood huddled beside gorgeous villas surrounded by security fencing and an array of floodlights.

Goats wandered near abandoned cars sitting on the side of the road on concrete blocks, hoods up and wheels gone. Small farms blended in with tall forests and swampland bracketed by a shoreline covered with tropical palms waving in the ever-present breeze.

They passed through small seaside towns with homemade bars emblazoned with bright hand-painted logos, crowded shops and iron-grated gas stations and grocery stores.

Outside the towns were long stretches of shoreline covered with construction projects. Mostly hurricane-leveled villas being rebuilt or brand-new resorts going up.

And then there were the isolated hillside communities winding around narrow dirt roads in a cluttered march down to the sea. As Beckett explained to the Executioner, these remote territories were the favored targets of Forca Militar, distant places where they could conduct their business undetected. Or so they thought.

Beckett's men had been gathering intelligence on the new underground network ever since it hit the shores.

"They made a lot of enemies when they first set up shop here," the Jamaican stated. "That's how we found out about them. Tips from some ganja gangs who have a righteous sense of things." He spoke matter-of-factly about the drug groups, many of them considering ganja a sacred thing and herb traffic a holy calling. Though the gangs often had shoot-'em-ups among themselves, there were long-lasting truces, codes and rules to follow.

Until Forca Militar broke them all.

When the Brazilians first moved in, they recruited some Jamaicans they'd dealt with previously in the drug trade. Then they gradually infiltrated the operation until they could replace key men with their own people. Soon the locals were on the outs, except when it came time to be offered up to rival gangs or to the law. Jamaicans were the first to go when the law breathed down their neck.

Anyone who informed on Forca Militar soon found himself dead and gone, but not forgotten. The Brazilian guerrillas made grisly examples of their enemies. And though they lost plenty of their own people, Forca Militar always brought in more reinforcements. With the reinforcements came more money, more drugs, more guns—everything needed to become a powerful force.

But now the counterforce was riding against them.

At speeds up to fifty miles an hour the bus carried the Jamaican security team up a winding road. It turned onto a narrow drive over a flat stretch of land where a small private cliffside "resort" looked out over the sea.

Complete with a uniformed staff, the small open-air hotel had begun operating in the area shortly after Forca Militar arrived. It catered to an exclusive clientele of police and security personnel who were all too glad to maintain their covers as well-off guests while they used the site as a safehouse and command post.

Beckett took him to the fenced-off edge of the landscaped grounds and pointed to the blue sea below. "There's our target," he said, indicating a cluster of houses off to the south. It was a heavily wooded area tilting toward a deserted beach with a handful of docks.

"Looks quiet," Bolan observed.

"In the daytime, yes," Beckett agreed. "But tonight the invasion begins. Forca Militar is on the move."

"Your intelligence is that good?"

A broad smile creased the security man's face. He nodded slightly and said, "We know everything that goes on down there. You might say we have a good-neighbor policy."

Later that night the good neighbors had some friends over. In ones and twos Jamaican security operatives filtered into the hillside home they'd maintained right in the heart of the Forca Militar outpost. The "neighbors" had played the parts of tough, scarred veterans of underworld wars. Easy enough roles to play since they'd fought that war for years. But they fought it on the same side as Sydney Beckett.

THE BRAZILIAN ENVOY cruised toward shore aboard a dark blue powerboat with outsize twin engines growling on low throttle.

His name was Cristobal Cavaros, and his diplomatic immunity came in the form of the short-barreled Uru submachine gun hanging like a 9 mm amulet from his stout, bell-shaped frame.

As sea spray fell all around him, the portly Brazilian gazed on the shore with the eyes of a conqueror.

It was a momentous occasion. And it was entirely in his hands, entrusted to him by the Ambassador himself, Antonio Moura.

Another page in the secret history of Forca Militar was about to be written. This would be remembered as the day Cristobal Cavaros brought in the hugest cache yet, a veritable armory that would soon claim the island for Forca Militar.

Farther out in the bay several more boats gathered like a school of sharks around the mother ship that sailed the waters off Jamaica's northern coast. It was a tramp freighter from Brazil that had long worked the Caribbean routes, carrying coffee, lumber, fruit, and most recently, a clandestine cargo.

The flotilla of boats readying to service the freighter were souped-up speedboats with the kind of deep decks favored by Forca Militar for running in contraband. There was nothing subtle about them. They were built for speed, attack and evasion.

Cavaros stood as the wheelman piloted the craft toward the M-shaped docks flanking an old but sturdy boat house. Standing a short distance uphill from the dock was a steeple-topped house with a slanting roof of weathered cedar, a church with armed chaplains holding late-night services.

With a soft-footed leap to the dock, almost graceful for a man of his bulk, Cavaros headed toward "the churchmen," as he called the Jamaican and Brazilian cohorts who lived there and in the surrounding houses.

He felt little apprehension as he ascended toward the Forca Militar haven a few steps ahead of his bodyguards.

The area was a stronghold of churchmen who'd gradually taken over this stretch of beach, displacing many of the original homeowners by using a combination of cash and threats.

The churchmen were on their way to becoming an underground aristocracy, and after this night's shipment they would be even more powerful, an auxiliary army at the beck and call of Forca Militar.

A sudden breeze raised the hairs on the back of Cavaros's neck as he reached the first gray slate tile of the walkway that led to the church.

The breeze came not from the sea but from the soul. Instincts that kept him alive for so long in the international arena were whispering to him again.

He stopped dead in his tracks and looked hard at the steepled dwelling. Shadowed faces looked back at him from the dimly lighted curtained windows. Then he looked up at the string of houses built into the hillside. Now they seemed too quiet, too safe. Lastly he looked at the woods that curved around the church itself.

"What's the matter?" Jorge asked, stepping in front of him. A towering Brazilian with a broad back and shoulders forged in Amazon mines, Jorge had a will that equaled his strength. He thought he could chase anything away simply by looking at it. Most of the time he was right.

"I hear a voice," Cavaros said, tapping the side of his head. "The voice of experience."

"What's it say?"

"It says Jorge is the best man to have with you on a night like this." He nodded toward the woods. "Check that out. See if there are any unexpected guests attending the services."

As the towering Brazilian headed toward the dark shadows of the woods, the second bodyguard stood beside Cavaros like a guard dog silently told to heel. His gaze swiveled from left to right, then back again, searching for enemies.

But he saw none.

Neither did Jorge, who returned from the woods and shook his head. "Nothing there."

Cavaros nodded. The sixth sense wasn't always accurate. Sometimes it lied, fooled by nerves. "Very well," he said. "Let us go worship at the altar." The others laughed, eager to join him at the altar of money and power.

There was little at risk, even if some authorities were in the area. The boat that brought the envoy and his men ashore held no cargo. The other boats would bring in the cargo only after Cavaros signaled it was safe.

A pillar of light spilled onto the walkway as the door slowly opened at their approach. Two men stood in the doorway, Garcilaso, the Forca Militar liaison with the local crew, and Preacher, the black-shirted Jamaican crew chief who studied Cavaros as if he were something that washed ashore and wasn't worth keeping.

Beyond them a roomful of churchgoers sat around fingering rapid-fire weaponry instead of rosaries.

Cavaros parked one bodyguard in the front room and drifted toward the kitchen for a sit-down with Garcilaso and the Preacher. Jorge entered the room first, then moved off to the side while the others sat at a long trestle-top table scarred with bottle rings and ash burns.

"Muscle waits outside," Preacher said, gesturing his head toward the Brazilian bodyguard. "Priests only tonight."

Cavaros met his gaze, sighed and shook his head. "He stays. If you didn't partake of your sacraments so much, you'd know that."

"No ganja here. Not till it's over. Anyway, just taking precautions like you say. Security."

"Jorge *is* my security," Cavaros replied. "There's little he doesn't know about our operations. And he's a lot more than muscle. He's my right hand. You should find such a man. Someone you can trust."

The Jamaican glanced at Garcilaso and smiled. "Luck has not been with me in that regard."

Garcilaso returned the thin smile. It was obvious to both sides that Preacher was walking a barbed-wire tightrope. While the arrangement with Forca Militar gave him more power and influence, it also gave him more enemies in the Jamaican underworld. And if the heat ever came down, he was in for a scorching.

"On to business," Cavaros stated. "Any problems?"

"No problem ever," Preacher said, his voice dignified, his eyes clear and challenging. "Not with my people."

Cavaros nodded. To a man in Preacher's situation, "no problem" could mean anything. Whether it was a shoot-out or a soiree, it was all the same to him. He was ready to face it. "And you, Garcilaso, is that the way you see it?"

The Brazilian agreed. "Nothing out of place. Everything in place," he replied. "The people, the transportation, the customers. Tonight we make our name as the organization to do business with."

"Yes," Cavaros said. "Once the arms come in, the power, glory and the word of this little church will spread like lightning. At least that's the plan."

The Jamaican sensed his hesitancy. "We're waiting for your benediction," he said.

Cavaros's fleshy hands clapped together, then opened slightly while he stared at them, as if he could divine the contents, as if the future were written in his hands. "There *is* something bothering me," he admitted. "Despite your assurances, I have this feeling that all is not as calm as you say. That we are being watched."

Garcilaso shook his head from side to side. "No. Impossible. Our people are the only ones doing the watching. No one else would dare move against us. We're ready."

Cavaros shrugged. "I will take your word, Garcilaso. But remember, our lives depend upon this guarantee of yours. Your life especially."

"There's nothing to fear."

"It is done," Cavaros said.

*"IT IS DONE."*

The words echoed from the small black speaker in the house halfway up the hill, set back off the dirt road. It was a whitewashed concrete structure with an excellent view of the docks, and through a webbing of carefully trimmed trees, a view of the church.

Sydney Beckett glanced at the men gathered around him. "Like the man says, 'It is done.' We're on, gentlemen."

Along with the undercover surveillance unit stationed in the house, the "gentlemen" included a strike team of Jamaican Federal Police, agents from the Customs Enforcement Branch, and Beckett's own recruits from the Jamaican Defence Force.

They were armed with a variety of submachine guns, riot guns and night-vision devices. Bolan was armed with his 93-R Beretta. "All the comforts of home," Beckett had said when he handed over the 9 mm weapon shortly after the Executioner's arrival at the hotel command post. It had been shipped through covert channels along with some of Bolan's other gear.

Though the warrior was familiar with most of the modern weaponry available and could use it when necessary, it never hurt to use one that he was familiar with and could instinctively depend upon.

"All right," Beckett said. "Let's go over it one more time." He ran a check of all the units and the parts they would play during the Forca Militar strike. His people were spread out along the upper reaches of the hillside, ready to contain the operation and seal off the area from the outside world.

Beckett stressed the need to go all-out. Once the operation started, silence wasn't top on his list. Impact was.

"Give it all you got," he stated. "We don't want any more innocent blood shed here. Too many people just trying to get by as it is. Too much suffering. They don't need more bullets ripping apart their houses. They need to know we are on duty and they can count on us. Make that loud and clear."

The operation would be loud enough to be heard around the world. Beckett wanted to let all comers know that Jamaica wouldn't tolerate a private army. Not here. Not elsewhere in the Caribbean. They'd proved that when their troops formed the bulk of the RSS units that helped squash the Trinidad-Tobago coup.

Tonight they were handling things their way.

Beckett's forces would take care of the ground troops. The Jamaican coast guard would take care of the freighters and the powerboats. And farther out there in the night were U.S. surveillance planes ready to track any Forca Militar boats that broke out of the field of containment.

A half hour later, a flurry of voices from the bugged churchhouse suddenly blared from the receiver.

"Now it starts," Beckett said. "And we finish them."

# 7

Bright cyclopean eyes slashed the darkness above the sea as the first powerboats made their run.

Loaded with cargo, the sleek black hulls moved like arrowheads as they chopped across the water in unison. As they neared the shore it looked like an invading force.

They dimmed their lights at the end of the run and cruised into the shelter of the boat house where the off-loaders waited for them.

Like a fireman's water brigade the churchgoers moved the crates from the boats onto bulky shoulders, and then up to the houses on the hill.

Rifles, grenades, launchers, submachine guns, explosives and detonators—enough to outfit a small army.

Cavaros watched the off-loaders with a wary eye, still unsettled by his earlier premonitions.

He and Garcilaso shouted orders to the crew who already worked with an urgency of their own, all of them determined to get it over with as soon as possible.

The off-loading was completed just like the Jamaican boss had promised, with no problems at all.

Until artificial daylight blazed down on them from the dark hills above.

Two choppers swooped into the area, their huge spotlights illuminating the ground below.

They came in like angry mutant wasps, buzzing and harassing the Forca Militar troops, who scattered like ants.

Cristobal Cavaros screamed orders for the men to stop, but they scrambled in all directions. Some headed for cover, while others stood stock-still like nocturnal prey hypnotized by the brilliant blazing light.

A moment ago they had been invincible, certain no one would dare move against them. But that illusion was quickly chopped into smoke by the rotorwash of the night-flying Westland Gazelles.

The lead chopper hovered above the hardmen, armed with antipersonnel rockets, missiles, miniguns, and just as importantly, a loudspeaker that boomed the pilot's warning down to them like the voice of God above.

It demanded immediate surrender.

The second chopper flew in a circular pattern, its searchlight tracing a no-man's-land around the perimeter of the drop site.

And in those eternal seconds, the men of the Forca Militar realized that before they could ever hope to take control of the island, there was a real army they had to deal with.

"Shoot! Shoot!" Cavaros shouted, grabbing at the men from the powerboat crews who were sprinting for the docks in panic. But he had little luck. In the bedlam of sound and fury raining upon them, the men had one thing in mind—get to their boats and get away.

PREACHER STOOD in front of the main house taking in the situation. From what he could see it was bad news. And he'd been around long enough to know that what he couldn't see was just as bad.

This wasn't a random flyby. It was the first nail driven by the hammer. The hammer was wielded by the full might of the Jamaican Defence Force, and the nail was pointed right at the Preacher's head. They knew all about him, and if they didn't get him now they could always get him later.

A circle of bright light that was filled with swirling debris fell upon Preacher, illuminating him like a dancer on stage—in front of a hostile audience.

He raised one hand to shield his eyes from the light and from the dizzying activity going on around him. There was too much running and screaming for his mind to take in.

The voice boomed once again from the chopper, telling Preacher to throw down his weapons.

Preacher's men looked to him for direction, ready to fire their weapons at his say-so. He glanced at their faces and saw nothing but dead men.

War was one thing. Mass suicide another. Preacher glanced at the men around him. No escape for him. No escape for them.

"Throw them down," he ordered, "and walk away."

He dropped his own submachine gun to the ground, initiating a sequence of guns thudding onto dirt as most of the Jamaicans followed his example.

Preacher was almost at the side of the house, warily stepping backward, when the bullet stream ripped through him and knocked him to his knees.

The fire came from someone on the ground.

Cristobal Cavaros.

The Brazilian's Uru submachine gun continued to chatter loudly, breaking the trance everyone had fallen into.

Preacher lurched toward the church house, his right shoulder a mass of bleeding and torn flesh. His good hand twisted behind him and freed the pistol holstered at the small of his back. As he crumpled forward, Preacher snaked his arm flat out, balanced the butt of the automatic on the hard ground and squeezed off a shot at Cavaros.

The round caught a man right in his chest, but not the Brazilian. One of his bodyguards had stepped in front of him, then flew backward with a look of fatal surprise on his face and a 9 mm hole punched through his heart.

Before he could squeeze the trigger again, a chill swept through Preacher, tugging him into unconsciousness.

Cavaros was still screaming and shouting to the band of Brazilian and Jamaican gunners. "Fight! Dammit! Fight them!" He sprayed the ground in all directions with gunfire, cutting off the churchmen just as they'd been about to vanish into the woods.

No desertion, no mutiny, no surrender would be tolerated by the Forca Militar envoy.

Jorge appeared beside Cavaros, training his submachine gun on the copter. He pulled the trigger, and a burst of autofire chinked into the armored cabin.

The gunfire increased as the rest of the Brazilians opened up, many of them whirling around from their flights toward the shore long enough to squeeze off a burst at the nearest chopper.

Once again the Jamaicans were caught on the razor edge. Because of the Brazilian resistance, battle was coming to them whether they wanted it or not. Most of them retrieved their guns while others headed for the woods.

That's when Armageddon fell.

Sheets of lead drilled down from the sky in a deadly hail as both choppers opened up. Miniguns blazed from the Gazelle, crashing and chopping into the trees, into the church, into the ranks of the Forca Militar.

Windows burst and doorframes fell, obliterated by the barrage. While their stronghold collapsed around them, the churchmen returned fire or fled, depending on which instinct screamed loudest in their minds.

The second Gazelle flew just offshore, strafing the docks and the powerboats with minigun and 20 mm cannon fire. One after the other the boats went up like fireworks as the heavy-metal barrage punched holes into their hulls and engines.

Two of the boats headed out to sea, but their bullet-riddled hulls were already taking on water. The Gazelle easily caught up to them, banking slightly and flying right behind them, spotlight pinning them against the dark sea.

The boats continued their flight even when the water-heavy hulls began to sink under the waves like high-speed sieves.

As the black shadow of the Gazelle closed in on the nearest boat, its tortured engines growling like a wounded animal, a Forca Militar gunman stitched the night with autofire.

He got only one chance to fire at the helicopter before a stream of 20 mm lightning bolts shredded the fuel-spitting outboard engines.

For a moment there was calm, then chaos reigned as the ignited fuel sent a fireball of flame whipping through the boat engulfing the vessel and its occupants before the explosion hurtled metal and flesh into the air like confetti.

The message was received loud and clear by the two-man crew in the second boat.

They cut their engines, tossed their weapons overboard and raised their hands as the Gazelle hit them with the spotlight.

It was the wisest move.

Even if the guerrillas had continued their run toward the open sea, they never would have made it. The Jamaican coast guard cutters were slashing across the bay, descending on the mother ship and sealing off all avenues of escape.

MEN IN BLACK FATIGUES and flak jackets spilled from the sliding door on the far side of the helicopter. A door gunner on the other side fired a steady stream of rounds, keeping the surprised Forca Militar hardmen at bay.

Other members of the assault team were also on the move, streaming through the woods, cordoning off the Jamaican and Brazilian gunmen.

As soon as the choppers had swept into the area and given the Militar gang a chance to surrender, the security teams were moving into action, filtering out from the safehouse and from positions farther uphill along the dirt road that led down into the settlement.

By the time the confrontation heated up and the first shots were fired, Sydney Beckett's covert strike force was in place. The panicked Forca Militar gunners believed that the woods offered them asylum.

The first volley of gunfire from the trees convinced them otherwise.

Lead drilled into the onrushing crowd of the guerrillas, and the first wave went down, their screams of pain drowned out by the chaotic chatter of 9 mm autofire.

The second wave of guerrillas paused, caught between the deadly ambush in the woods and a steady stream of rounds from the copter crew.

In the midst of the Forca Militar gunners moved the unmistakable stout form of Cristobal Cavaros. Like a man possessed, he urged them on in a suicidal assault. He fired his submachine gun wildly, slamming another magazine home while he directed fire from the others.

A spear-point attack followed as the gunmen rallied behind Cavaros, all of them directing their fire into the same wooded area.

Three of Beckett's men fell dead from the concentrated barrage. Two others were wounded, dropping to the ground like toppled trees.

The path to freedom was momentarily clear.

With Cavaros in the lead, the Forca Militar survivors headed for the breach. By the time they reached cover, they'd lost half a dozen more men to flanking fire.

But they made it into the woods.

Now it was every man for himself.

THE MAN IN BLACK DIVED forward as two guerrillas thrashed through the brush ten feet away from him. One of the gunmen turned at the movement, his submachine gun starting to track on the Executioner.

Bolan fired a 3-round burst and kept rolling. His trio of 9 mm slugs caught the guerrilla head-on, a fountain of blood cascading down his body.

The burst from the expiring gunman drilled into a tree a foot above Bolan's head. Then, continuing on momentum, the guerrilla toppled forward, his limbs wrapping around a sapling in a dead embrace.

"Garcilaso!" shouted the second man as his comrade fell. He turned toward Bolan's position.

The Executioner hurried through the brush, knowing a firestorm would burn hot on his heels. A full clip of ammo peppered the woods around him, lagging a few crucial seconds behind the warrior's trail.

Bolan homed in on the second man, then took him out of play with a short burst. The man dropped to the ground without a sound.

All around came the sounds of men screaming, thrashing in the woods, cursing, unloading lead and loading it just as quickly. Like magnets, the security team was drawn toward the fleeing Forca Militar gunners.

The skirmish line changed back and forth in serpentine motion as both sides searched the darkness for the enemy.

While most of the Jamaican security men kept in close contact with the guerrillas, Bolan and a handful of commandos circled back in a prearranged movement, cutting through the darkness until they were directly in line of the advancing Forca Militar troops.

One of the Jamaican churchmen burst into the kill zone, high-kicking it over the snagging vines that crawled along the ground.

"Freeze!" Beckett shouted, stepping out from cover and tracking the Jamaican with a Colt AR-15.

The gunman measured the distance between life and death. There were only a few feet between him and cover, a split-second chance for freedom.

He took the chance, continuing his flight while bearing his automatic on Beckett.

Beckett blew him away with a rapid burst that hammered him off to one side, then dropped him into the greenery.

Three men headed straight for Bolan, bounding like wild deer through the woods. They were in flight, but not defenseless. Each man carried a submachine gun.

The gunner in the lead was gargantuan, his massive bulk propelled by a sheer force of will and meanness that let him outdistance most of the younger and leaner guerrillas. Cristobal Cavaros. Next to him was a much taller man, the bodyguard named Jorge. And on the side closer to Bolan was a knife-thin hardman who hurdled through the clinging undergrowth with animal grace.

The third man also had feral instincts.

Even before the Executioner moved, the man turned his way, already firing the submachine gun, muzzle-flashes winking in the darkness.

But Bolan had him in his own sights, tracking him by instinct. As soon as the man opened up, the warrior replied with a burst from the Beretta.

The gunner dropped the subgun as if it were on fire, then he pressed his hands across the bullet wounds in his chest, intent on staunching the blood. As he fell to his knees, he looked around for the man in black, then dropped face-first into the cold earth.

Both Cavaros and Jorge stopped at the same time, ducking back into cover and hosing the tree line with automatic gunfire.

The onslaught caused Bolan to drop low again, but he managed to squeeze off three rounds that caught Jorge as he was edging around a tree trunk. The burst stitched his right leg, spinning him and taking him out of the action.

Behind the men came the sounds of a full-scale battle as the rest of the security team closed in on Forca Militar.

Cavaros looked behind him, then looked at Jorge, who was crumpled on the ground.

"Jorge," the Brazilian said. "Always at my side." He stepped closer. "But Forca Militar must survive," he said, pointing his gun at the wounded bodyguard's head. "It has to be this way."

Bolan emerged from the trees then, training the Beretta on Cavaros. The stout man made an easy target from this range. He shouted once, getting the Brazilian's attention.

Cavaros looked up and swung around his weapon. Before he could get off a shot Bolan cut him down with a single head shot from the Beretta.

"WELCOME TO THE HOTEL," Sydney Beckett said, looking down at the bandaged giant whose right arm and leg were wrapped in white. His left arm and leg were wrapped in cuffs attached to the side rail of the hospital bed.

Jorge opened his eyes and looked around the room, taking in the circle of armed men, his eyes pausing for a moment when he saw Mack Bolan.

"What kind of hotel is this?" the Brazilian bodyguard asked.

"A very secret one," Beckett replied. "Very discreet. No guest list. No interruptions from the outside world."

Jorge nodded.

He'd been in the underground long enough to realize he was in a safehouse and that special measures had to be taken when a man in his position was captured by the other side. More than once he'd been the one who took that special measure with one of Cavaros's prisoners.

"What do you want?" Jorge asked.

The bearded Jamaican security chief spoke softly, as if this were just another meeting, rather than an interrogation, that they were all on the same side and there was no question of the outcome. Jorge would talk. It was as simple as that.

Beckett told him of the final outcome of the battle, the number of living, the number of dead. The seizure of the mother ship and the roundup of the Jamaican and Brazilian guerrillas.

"Skip the final score," Jorge said. "Just tell me what you want."

"Very well," Beckett replied. "We in Jamaica do not want much from you. Enough blood has already been spilled here. We have made our statement loud and clear. Perhaps loud enough to be heard all the way back to Manaus, near your headquarters on the Amazon. For all effective purposes, here on the island Forca Militar has been disbanded."

It came as no surprise to the prisoner who'd been in the thick of battle, seeing men fall around him.

"Trust me when I tell you all through the Caribbean we are rolling back similar operations of your people," Beckett continued. "Sharing intelligence *and* troops. Whatever is required, we will provide it. The Regional Security System does not play around."

Jorge grimaced from the pain that racked his right arm and leg.

"As you've noticed," Beckett added.

Jorge nodded. His face was covered with sweat. The medication was starting to wear off, and his wounds were starting to ache. It was impossible to hide his discomfort. "Dammit! Just tell me what you want."

Beckett nodded toward Bolan. "He requests your services. Perhaps you remember him. He's the man who shot you in the first place. I think he might be interested in finishing the job. Perhaps not. After all, he is the man who prevented your own leader from silencing you. You are aware of that?"

The wounded man looked up at the ceiling, no doubt reviewing the memory of Cristobal Cavaros pointing a weapon at his head. "He wanted to preserve the secrets of the organization."

"By killing you," Beckett said. He nodded to one of his security men, who stepped over to the hospital bed and unlocked the cuffs.

Jorge laughed weakly, looking down at his wounded arm and leg. "So," he said, "you don't think I'm at risk of escaping."

Beckett smiled. "Oh, you're still at risk," he said, stepping over to the floor-to-ceiling drapes of the room and pulling them wide open to reveal sliding glass doors. The view through the glass showed manicured green lawns rolling down to the cliff that looked over the sea green Caribbean.

As if he were admiring the view, Beckett said, "Some of our previous guests didn't like the arrangements we made for them here. They escaped by jumping off that cliff."

Jorge studied the view. "Who?"

"They shall remain nameless. As I said, we're very discreet about who checks in—and who checks out."

Beckett gestured to his men. Without another look at the wounded man, who for all purposes was invisible to them, they followed Beckett out of the room.

Bolan stepped close to the bed, approaching from the wounded side. He'd seen men in worse shape than Jorge do a lot of damage to the unwary.

"First," the warrior said, "I'll tell you what *I* know." He mentioned how the church house was bugged by Jamaican security, how they overheard the details of Forca Militar and Jorge's place in it. As the right-hand man of Cristobal Cavaros, the bodyguard had to have knowledge of the underground army's operations across Brazil and their contacts in the business community and the underworld. A man who traveled with an upper-echelon Forca Militar commander would know the locations of guerrilla strongholds, weapons caches, and most important, for Bolan, where the American prisoners were held if they were still alive.

Jorge's eyes remained impassive.

Bolan touched him on the shoulder. "Before we start," he said, "I have one question that will decide whether I have anything else to say to you. Do you understand?"

Jorge looked into the eyes of the Executioner and saw a darkness that could wrap around him like a shroud.

Despite all the noble talk of brotherhood, the solidarity of the Forca Militar and the kinship of revolutionaries, Jorge had seen those sentiments blown away by the barrel of Cristobal Cavaros's gun.

Even without pulling the trigger, Cavaros had killed the last shred of loyalty Jorge might have had. In the end there was only one man who claimed Jorge's ultimate loyalty. Himself.

"And now the question," Bolan said. "Do you want to walk out of this room alive?"

Jorge answered yes, and started to talk.

**8**

Another layer of scorched red skin peeled from the American's shoulders as he swung the machete into the thick stalk of sugarcane.

It didn't go all the way through. The stalk snapped and leaned drunkenly, requiring two more swings of the machete before it broke off clean.

He could tell the workday was almost over for him. His swings fell weakly on the stalks and his lungs grew congested with cane dust. His right arm rose again, the heavy blade arcing down in mind-numbing repetition.

A hot dry breeze swept through the row of cane stalks that imprisoned him as surely as any iron bars.

Around him he heard the thwack and chop of other machetes slicing through the stalks, wielded by other men under the thumb of Forca Militar.

An eternity ago, Lawrence Adams had been six feet, two hundred pounds. The height remained, but the weight was dwindling. His captives gave him just enough food to stay alive. That, plus whatever food he could steal, had transformed his once healthy body into that of a scarecrow.

The musculature he once had was little more than a memory now, but it was a memory kept alive by will-power. Will was like muscle. It had to be exercised or it would be lost.

Just like the others were lost.

For all he knew, all but two of them were dead. Forca Militar had killed the other three long ago.

Unless he continued fighting, even if it was only in his mind, Lawrence Adams knew he would also be lost.

There wasn't a single day since his capture that the black shroud of despair hadn't descended. It came most often at the end of the day when his mind was free from forced labor and he collapsed on his rotting cot in his decrepit hut. His world was reduced to this, a foul-smelling hovel. And outside the huts were the voices of the guardians, the Forca Militar sentries who taunted him wherever he went. Like a target in an arcade, their gun barrels followed him like metal eyes.

Vermin-ridden, feverish, exhausted, he'd been shunted from one place to another by boat, by long arduous walks through the jungle, by bone-rattling rides in jeep convoys.

His captors delighted in his plight, promising that he would spend the rest of his days serving those whom he sought to destroy. Other days they told him he would be ransomed soon and a deal was in the works. But the deal was always a mirage.

Still other times he was told they would make an example of him, a cause célèbre. If Forca Militar activities were ever exposed, they would blame it all on American intervention and CIA subterfuge. Whenever the time was right, they could trot him out as living proof of Yankee imperialism, a secret warrior who was not so secret anymore.

Sometimes when Adams thought of the range of the underground organization, he almost lost hope. From Marajó Island to Manaus—the route they'd taken up the Amazon—Forca Militar had several strongholds, and safehouses wherever they required. They simply moved into small towns and pressured the inhabitants to cooperate. When the alternative was death, cooperation was almost universal.

Forca Militar had connections that ran south into the interior of the Amazon rain forest. They had strike teams based in the north, reaching as far as the Venezuelan border. The teams handled weapons, coke and cannabis transfers. They also bankrolled illegal gold-mining operations and preyed on any independent operators who dared to venture into *their* illegal domain.

From the conversations Adams had with others trapped in the Forca Militar net, he knew they had connections in the cities and in the government.

Forca Militar guerrillas never tired of talking about his capture. It gave their army a sense of legitimacy. After all, they'd gone against the best the U.S. had to offer and they'd won.

And no one had come for him.

Adams knew that was part of the deal, part of the risk he took when he'd signed to take part in covert ops. But in the back of his mind there was always a glimmer of hope that someone, somewhere, was looking for him.

THE ARTERY that brought life to Rio de Janeiro's business district was Avenida Rio Branco. Money, securities and gemstone fortunes flowed at dizzying speeds in and out of the banks and corporate head quarters housed in granite-and-glass high rises.

Throughout the day couriers, local power brokers and international businessmen moved along the white-and-black-tiled sidewalks like pieces on a board game.

But the main players of the international Monopoly game sat undisturbed in plush corporate aeries high above the street. Some of them were powerful, well-respected international CEOs. Others were equally powerful, and though not exactly respected, they were certainly feared. To them corporate warfare was something to be taken literally. The casualties were hushed up, but the body counts were very real.

Chief among the feared CEOs was Martin Machado. A small man with big dreams, he often held court in his tinted glass-and-steel tower in the middle of Avenida Rio Branco. Known as Castelo dos Machado, the tower complex was the secret heart and soul of Forca Militar, which was only one of its profitable enterprises.

Machado's silver hair gave him a benevolent, almost paternal look. But like his business practices, his looks were deceiving. Many a protégé of Martin Machado found out firsthand that he was capable of murder if the protégé became too much of a threat to his power.

Machado liked his subordinates to be competent, ruthless and several shades less clever than he. He also liked them to be successful, which was why Antonio Moura, the Forca Militar ambassador, now stood before him and the other solemn members of the council who'd gathered to hear his confession, his crimes against the invisible empire.

Moura stood mutely in front of them, politely looking straight ahead while the men talked among themselves.

Despite everything at stake—his life—Moura acted perfectly at ease in the regal surroundings.

The Ambassador had left his combat fatigues behind him in the jungles near Manaus. Today he wore a black business suit tailored to his wide shoulders and slim waist. His hair was freshly cut, and his tanned body completely massaged. He had just spent the early afternoon aboard one of the company yachts in the restorative arms of a company blonde, a bright young icebreaker kept on hand to cement business deals with newcomers.

All in all, he'd had everything a condemned man could want on his last day.

The councillors conferred among themselves, ignoring Moura.

He followed his instincts, remaining silent and looking straight ahead, trying to keep his mind off the opulent display of power arrayed against him.

The meeting was being held in a top-floor suite of Castelo dos Machado in a cream-colored room with curtained windows. The curtains were always drawn at these summit meetings to prevent eavesdropping from laser mikes that might be aimed at the windows to pick up the vibrations of their voices.

Security teams always swept the premises before the meetings convened. And then, in absolute secrecy, Martin Machado conducted the meeting like a head of state.

At the moment, Machado was seated at the center of a marble-topped conference table, its horseshoe shape providing seats for half a dozen men on each side of him. The gleaming gold surface was polished to a mirror-like shine, reflecting the somber faces of the men on the council.

The peers of Martin Machado.

Like their leader, most of them had military or intelligence pasts, from which they'd profited greatly. They'd made their first fortunes while supposedly in the service of their country. In the covert military and intelligence network they made contacts and contracts with suppliers from the business sector. They also exported restricted arms and military know-how to just about any country that could afford to pay for it.

Over the years they were recruited by Martin Machado, the former general who drew them into his orbit and kept them one step ahead of the firing squad. His short stature gave him a Napoleonic complex that won him rapid advancement and a host of enemies. Eventually, in order to escape the scandals and corruption that plagued Brazil's military government, Machado had been forced to leave the army. But years of preparation gave him a soft landing as he parachuted into a corporate network he'd secretly controlled for years. Coffee plantations, steel mills, ranches, chemical combines and military supply companies were some of the legal industries under the man's umbrella. He now held Antonio Moura's fate in his manicured hands.

"And now on to Antonio," Machado announced, raising his hand.

The others fell silent at the gesture.

Their eyes bore down on Antonio just as Machado's did, but none matched his in intensity. His eyebrows peaked rigidly as he studied the man before him like a creature of prey.

It was rumored among the more superstitious members of Machado's circle that he had the evil eye, that whoever he looked upon in wrath would soon come to a grisly end.

But that didn't mean it was supernatural. Machado had enough manpower to silence anyone he looked at cross-eyed.

"You know why you are here," Machado began.

Moura nodded.

"Enlighten us."

"The . . . difficulties in the Caribbean."

" 'Difficulties,' " Machado repeated. "Spoken like a true diplomat. It gladdens me to see that you have mastered the art of statecraft. But words are one thing. Difficulties another."

Machado suddenly leaned forward, his fist pounding on the table.

"Every newspaper in the Caribbean has splashed the Jamaican outrage across their pages, an outrage repeated throughout the islands. All of the people we put into place, all of the men we cultivated—all of that has gone up in smoke. Thanks to you."

Though Machado spoke calmly at first, he gradually worked himself up into a gale-force harangue, his face growing redder and redder. Then a stream of hate, blame and threats poured out.

The Ambassador stood his ground, impassively accepting the tirade. The details weren't news to him. Forca Militar's newest target territories were no longer under their control. Cristobal Cavaros, their main envoy, was killed in action. Others were dead or unaccounted for.

Forca Militar's foothold in the islands was knocked out with one concerted sweep. Now underworld gangs would fill the vacuum left by the guerrilla army's bloodied retreat.

American and Caribbean authorities had worked hand in hand to dismantle the network they'd put into place. From Jamaica down to Trinidad, the hold of Forca Militar was broken.

Taken by itself it was a major setback for the Ambassador. Following so closely on the debacle of the botched ransom exchange for Clorinda Sertano, it was a nearly fatal setback.

And now the recently departed souls of Forca Militar's men hung heavy around Moura's neck, a ghostly necklace that could very well choke him.

"Until today our role has been secret," Machado said. "But now the finger is pointing at us. Reporters in the Caribbean and the United States talk of a subversive organization from South America that was the source of all the carnage. Some of them go so far as to mention Brazil."

Moura waited silently. He nodded his head on cue, aware that they were playing the game of puppet and puppet master. His time to respond would come.

"Freedom fighting, revolution, subversion," Machado said. "It is all good business. Such a business demands weapons. It demands causes. It demands men who are willing to take chances and bend rules. Such men we have in abundance—inside our borders. And we almost had them outside our borders. Unfortunately that venture has come to an end.

And that is why we are here. It is time for us to decide if we have to redraw the map."

He looked coldly at Moura, making it clear the drawing would be done with a knife.

"Before making an adjustment regarding your position," Machado said, "we want to know what you have to say."

"Very well." Moura's voice sounded loud, clear and perversely eager. He stepped closer to the center of the table. Flanked by the gray vultures of Machado's secret cabinet, he looked from face to face and said, "I say it is all nonsense."

He waited for the shock to subside and the murmuring to begin. Of them all, only Martin Machado seemed unruffled. He had a somewhat pleased look on his face. Like a Caesar of old, Machado often rewarded defiance with great fortune or execution.

"Nonsense, Antonio? Our council comes to nonsense?"

"Nothing but. When it comes to matters you know of—finance, logistics, delegation and networking—your council is as good as gold. But out there—" he pointed toward the curtained window "—out there it's another world, one that has grown unfamiliar to you. It is a world populated by killers, traitors and heroes. Anything can happen in such a world. Unfortunately it happened to us. This time. Next time will be different."

Machado nodded. "You think you can regain the lost territories."

"I'm already planning it," he replied.

Machado looked at the faces of his cabinet members. They were subtly gauging the general's mood, not committing themselves to condemn Moura until and unless their leader did.

"I hoped as much," the old man said. "But for the time being put your plan on hold. There is something else you must deal with."

"Whatever you wish," Moura said.

"Of course. And what I wish is for you to prove yourself capable of maintaining your position with Forca Militar when it comes under attack."

"Who would dare?"

Machado leaned forward, enjoying the torment of the Ambassador. Moura had been reprieved only to face another potentially fatal challenge. And for a moment he felt like a wild creature kept in Machado's menagerie, one pit bull to be thrown against another.

"The same people who moved against us in the Caribbean are still moving. They are coming down here to our own territory, Antonio. Now it is no longer a matter of expanding. It is a matter of holding on to what we have until these people are taken care of."

"Who are they?"

Machado nodded toward an intense black-bearded man to his right, a former counterintelligence officer who had all the charm of an inquisitioner, which earned him that nickname in Machado's circle.

"At this very moment Colonel Joaquim Almeiros is preparing a strike against Forca Militar," the intelligence man said. "He has assembled a team of Jaguars that is loyal only to him—for the most part. Working with him in this operation is an American agent named Michael Belasko."

"Never heard of him."

"Correct," the man said. "You never heard of him. You never saw him. Yet he is the same one who took out your people at Marajó Island and crushed your operation in Jamaica. We have reason to believe this is the man known as the Executioner."

Moura shrugged. "That is just a myth. A cover name used by several operatives. No one man could do what he's said to have done."

The concept wasn't new to any of the men in the room. It was standard practice in the covert community to assign victorious operations to one name, building up a legend so the very mention of that name would send a shudder through the opposition.

Machado nodded. "Perhaps. Perhaps not. A man with the right backing, training and the right cause...such a man could prevail. Unless he runs into a superior force. It is your obligation to make sure we are that force."

"If it is under my command," Moura replied.

"You have Forca Militar units at your disposal. Police and intelligence contacts. Assets in the army. Allies in the tribes. Do you think with all that we are capable of winning?"

"Yes."

"Of course, if this proves too much for you, we could return the American hostages, raising them from the dead if we have to. We could get down on our knees and beg for mercy from the Americans. Or perhaps we could all tie ropes around our necks and hang ourselves."

Moura shook his head. "Forca Militar will be victorious."

"Even against the Executioner?"

"Against anyone."

Machado nodded and sat back, looking once again like a CEO instead of a warlord. "Then prepare for war, Antonio."

The counterintelligence chieftain took over once again, filling Moura in on Colonel Almeiros's planned operation and on the alleged Executioner. According to their intelligence, several flights to Brazil had been booked for Michael Belasko. He would arrive either in Recife, Belém, São Paulo or Rio de Janeiro, then take another flight to Manaus, his ultimate destination. If things worked out, he would never make it there.

Regardless of whatever flight he took, Forca Militar would have operatives on the planes and at the airports. Joaquim Almeiros would be kept busy while they concentrated on the Executioner who would be shadowed wherever he went.

And the American would find out what happened to those who trespassed in the outlaw borders of Forca Militar.

**9**

Joaquim Almeiros wasn't there to meet Bolan at the airport at Manaus.

The warrior considered the alternatives as he waited near the revolving luggage rack. The Brazilian counterinsurgency specialist was either dead or he'd been finessed out of the situation by someone high up in the Forca Militar network.

Neither alternative was appealing.

Bolan searched the crowd surging around him. Other than a few fleeting glances, the casual stares of strangers meeting each other's eyes, no one seemed inordinately interested in him.

But his instincts spoke differently.

He was being watched, measured.

If this was a hit, his watchers would blend in with the horde of tourists and returning natives of Manaus. They would watch him until they could carry out the hit or maybe hand off the surveillance to another team. And then he would vanish like Joaquim Almeiros.

If he played into their hands.

Bolan was unarmed, but he wasn't unprepared.

He watched his luggage go around several times, while he pretended to search for it. The crowd gradually thinned out until only a dozen people remained. A few of them walked over to the airline's information booth to file a claim for lost luggage. Several more found theirs.

Only one unclaimed suitcase and three people remained—two men in dark suits and Bolan.

Neither man looked especially like a businessman. The taller one's arms were solemnly folded in front of him, one meaty paw nervously clenching the other. The second man paced idly, looking first at the luggage rack, then at Bolan, then at his companion. If not for the suddenly awkward situation, both men might have passed as everyday civilians to an untrained eye.

They tried not to look directly at Bolan, but he looked at them dead-on, memorizing their faces.

Then he picked up his suitcase, approached the taller of the two men and nodded toward the airline's information booth. "The woman over there can probably help you out with your luggage," he said. "Good luck."

The man's face turned to granite, his eyes to ice. He might not have been the brightest man in the world, but he knew when someone was making a fool of him.

Bolan walked away, knowing that from here on in a taste for vengeance would cloud the man's judgment.

A few minutes later Bolan stepped outside the passenger terminal and studied the line of taxis at the curb, his shadows right behind him, leaning against a wall near the entrance.

The Executioner knew that these men could be the least of his worries. Chances were that the airport was full of Forca Militar operatives. In a city with the population approaching one million people, the airport was thriving with activity—passengers, security men, drivers, baggage handlers. With that kind of chaos, the opposition could easily have a score of agents in place.

In this sea of uncertainty one thing was guaranteed—his shadows weren't alone.

Nor was Bolan.

After a few minutes' wait he saw a titanium-white Mercedes gleaming in the bright afternoon sunlight as it cruised down the roadway. It pulled up behind the line of taxis, and a black man in denim jeans and short-sleeve shirt slid out from behind the wheel. He walked behind the car and leaned against the trunk, glancing at the entrance.

The Executioner's backup had arrived.

It was Jacques, the DEA agent who'd been attached to the Justice Department operation since the brainstorming session in Miami. While the Executioner was busy spearheading the Caribbean phase of the operation, Jacques had come down to Brazil to coordinate Brognola's "civilian" support apparatus in the Amazon.

It was a typical fallback operation. Under the circumstances Bolan and Brognola had opted for expanding their covert presence in the area. In a worst-case scenario the Executioner could still operate independently of Brazilian support. They trusted Almeiros completely, but even so, the Jaguar commander was in a position of high risk. If the men got whacked there were damn few locals Bolan could call on for help.

The warrior turned back to the two hardmen, smiling thinly as he approached them. "You guys need a ride?" he asked.

Both men glared at him. The shorter one murmured something in a Portuguese dialect Bolan couldn't follow. But the kind of hatred that colored his face needed no translation. The other man refused the offer in halting English.

Bolan dropped the smile and reached inside his jacket as if a weapon were holstered under his shoulder. "It's not a question," he said, moving close, crowding them.

They stepped back, looking around for help. Their target wasn't following the scenario laid out for them. The look on his face made it clear that he was ready to force a showdown right there. They needed guidance.

It came in the person of a barrel-chested man with a short clipped mustache and a high-pitched voice who pushed through the glass doors where he'd been waiting and watching, overseeing the operation. "Mr.

Belasko! Mr. Belasko. I'm so glad I caught you in time..."

The heavy-handed surveillance team backed off at his approach and retreated through the entrance doors.

"You know me?" Bolan said.

"I know *of* you. Please forgive me for not meeting you earlier, but I was regrettably detained on security matters."

Bolan nodded. The man he'd smoked out was a lot smoother than the first baby-sitting team. For one thing, a suit wasn't alien to him. It was tailored to his powerful physique. His lean face was calm, and his gaze was clear and steady. He acted like a man of considerable wealth and will.

"Should I know you?" Bolan said.

"Rogerio Silva," the man replied, ushering the Executioner off to the side, away from the flow of people near the entrance. "Colonel Almeiros sent me in his place." His English was rapid but other than that, remarkably unaccented.

"What happened to him?"

Silva raised his hands. "A bureaucratic matter, no doubt. Something to do with transport and supply for the, eh, pending field operation."

"I see." Bolan listened to the stream of lies that flowed easily from the man's lips. Silva threw in enough talk of the operation to almost convince him that Almeiros had clued him in on it. It seemed genuine except for one thing. The arrangements that

Bolan and the Brazilian had previously worked out called for absolutely no outside interference.

Almeiros was adamant that under no circumstances would he send someone in his place. If he couldn't make it, for whatever reason, then Bolan was to head for an address near a botanical garden on the edge of the city.

"But you and I can get the ball rolling while we wait for Joaquim," Silva said. "I have a car waiting—"

"So do I."

Silva's eyes narrowed. "But I don't understand. I thought Joaquim was going to meet you here."

"Yes," Bolan replied. "I was informed on the plane that Joaquim was unable to meet me. Other arrangements were made."

"By whom?"

"Friends," the warrior stated.

"I see."

And now both men knew the other was lying, a cat-and-mouse game where each lie produced another. They were playing it on Silva's territory, but Bolan had no other choice. The only thing in his favor was that Silva probably wouldn't want to make a scene.

It was in his best interests to untangle Bolan from the surveillance web, get him safely away from the area, *then* eliminate him.

"Let me drive you to your hotel, then," Silva said. "Where are you staying?"

"With friends."

The Brazilian nodded. "I think you should tell me where. In case Joaquim has to get in touch with you."

"He already knows how. That's all been taken care of."

Silva stepped closer. It was obvious that he was eager for toe-to-toe diplomacy. He had about twenty pounds on Bolan, and he had the look of a man who didn't shy away from violence. In fact he was likely the type who savored it.

Bolan stood his ground, aware they played in a different league. Silva was a murderer, not an assassin. It was a crucial difference, and the Brazilian would be dead before he understood that.

"Mr. Belasko, I have the authority to command you to come with me. As a guest in my country—involved in a sensitive, possibly deadly, area—it would be best if you came with me freely."

"As a guest, I must decline your kind offer. If you need to get in touch with me, do it through Joaquim. He'll know where I am at all times. Now if you'll excuse me..." He picked up his suitcase and started to walk away.

"Wait!" Silva called, rushing to his side. "Mr. Belasko, you must realize it can be dangerous to walk alone—"

Bolan stopped and turned. He looked into the eyes of the Brazilian, and in that lucid gaze he saw a creature of prey about to devour his quarry.

"Unless you accompany me," Silva said, "I cannot be held responsible for your safety."

"Thanks for your concern. I'll take that chance."

He headed toward the white Mercedes, glancing once behind him to see a small crowd of not-so-secret agents flocking around their boss.

THE STREETS OF MANAUS were crowded with fast-moving traffic that wound through a maze of old European-style architecture built in the early 1900s when capitalist dreamers first carved the city out of the jungle and made their millions from the great rubber plantations.

In recent years modern office complexes sprouted up side by side with the ornate palatial facades. In some districts the steel towers dominated the skyline of Amazonas's capital city, casting spirelike shadows on the streets.

As a duty-free port city the streets were full of buyers and sellers of all stripes who came from all over Brazil to buy goods in mass quantities.

State-of-the-art computers, stereos, TVs, VCRs, bicycles and motorcycles were assembled from tax-free parts flown in by international companies.

One again Manaus was a boomtown, full of factories and service industries, hotels and luxury shops, produce stands and fish markets, and world-class restaurants to cater to the expensive whims of the elite.

It was a chaotic capital, a burgeoning Big Apple that attracted wealthy riverboat wanderers who journeyed a thousand miles up the Amazon River for a relatively safe taste of the wilderness. From there they could book cruises or safaris or settle in for the exotic pleasures of some of the high-rise luxury hotels.

It was a fairy-tale city on the edge of the jungle.

But, as the two men in the white Mercedes knew, every fairy tale had its share of monsters. For them the modern city was just as dangerous as the jungle surrounding it.

Several vehicles tailed the Mercedes like a wolf pack homing in on a single target in the herd, mimicking their motions as the vehicle traveled deeper into Manaus.

Jacques had forced them to give away the game by running stoplights and making last-minute turns onto narrow streets that he'd scouted beforehand.

"We got a four-car posse on our ass," Jacques said, looking unconcerned as he wheeled the Mercedes around a sharp corner, braking for a woman in a bright red dress with a string of small kids tagging along behind her.

"Four that we know of," Bolan replied. "This group goes in for overkill."

The black man nodded, then gestured at the glove compartment. "Just in case it gets heavy," he said, "there's your ticket out of here."

Bolan opened the compartment.

Inside was a compact 9 mm automatic, a Heckler & Koch P7 M-8 with a squeeze grip cocking mechanism. Along with the automatic pistol there were several magazines and a cutaway holster that clipped to the inside of his belt. The small but powerful weapon was only six and a half inches long and easily concealable.

The Executioner adjusted the rig under his suit jacket, making sure the metal bulk wouldn't be too obvious in public.

"Thanks," Bolan said, briefly glancing back through the rear window at their nearest tail. "Now I feel dressed for the occasion."

"In case you need a softer touch," Jacques said, "there's a hush puppy under the seat."

Bolan reached under the front seat, knowing what he would find. The weapon was a 9 mm stainless steel Navy Model 22 with a sound suppressor threaded onto the barrel. The automatic pistol had earned the nickname "hush puppy" as the weapon of choice for silencing guard dogs, or for that matter, two-legged mad dogs.

The Executioner placed the silenced weapon on the seat next to him, then pulled his suitcase from the back seat. He opened it up and packed away several spare magazines.

They drove several more blocks, long enough for the backup man to give Bolan a crash course in the housekeeping arrangements he'd set up in Manaus. Jacques had strung together a network of safehouses, phone message services, and a floating base of operations, a double-decker riverboat that he'd chartered for one month. It was anchored near the old harbor with a score of similar crafts.

"This is where we say goodbye," Jacques announced as he turned down a long narrow street bordered by swank shops and rows of double-parked cars. "I'll see you later, man." With a wrench of the wheel and a screech of brakes, Jacques sent the car into a controlled skid that came to a rocking sideways stop.

The Mercedes completely blocked all traffic.

Bolan pushed open the door and hurried into the street. He headed south as casually as a running man could, suitcase in his left hand, raincoat draped over his right arm.

Behind him he heard car doors slamming, brakes squealing and a chorus of inspired curses and threats.

Jacques's voice was right up there among them, as he got out of the car and bellowed at two burly men who ran up to him, screaming in his face. An instant later fists started to fly. One of the men went down hard. The other stopped screaming and started to back away from Jacques, who headed north up the street.

An army of Forca Militar operatives jumped from their cars and hurried down the street, their panicked and venom-charged faces reflecting in the glitzy storefront windows as they split up and went after the two refugees.

TEN MINUTES LATER, after drifting down several side streets, Bolan realized he hadn't broken out of the surveillance net.

Forca Militar had launched a massive operation in his honor, fielding teams on foot and in a fleet of cars.

They were well prepared, staying on him ever since Jacques tried the maneuver with the Mercedes. This was their territory. They knew their way around, and they knew they had their man at last.

It was easy to pick them out. They were the ones who were watching him but not watching him, never looking directly at him. Instead, their gazes floated past him, taking him in but quickly looking elsewhere.

That apparently random pattern marked the men as surveillance operatives. There were too many of them with wandering gazes for it to be coincidence.

The hit was going down.

Proof of that came from the faces of two men the Executioner had seen earlier, the pair of shadows he'd flushed out back at the airport baggage area. The familiar faces loomed out of the crowd coming toward him on the sidewalk.

It was payback time and they had a hard time hiding the anticipation from their stone-cold faces.

The two men closed ranks.

Bolan sensed a flurry of motion behind him from another team, and, threading its way through a slow-moving mass of cars, was yet another quartet of men on urgent business, crossing over to his side of the street.

Without breaking stride, the Executioner walked out into the street, narrowly avoiding a yellow Volkswagen taxi that screeched to a stop and lurched forward.

While the driver shook his fist and shouted obscen-
-ities, Bolan smacked a hand on the hood and vaulted
safely out of the way. Then he sprinted to the other
side of the street.

The quartet did an about-face. They too wandered
back over to the sidewalk behind Bolan. Other hardmen drifted toward the warrior in twos and threes,
though others stayed on the opposite side, hurrying
ahead to cut him off.

Bolan kept walking, his combat instincts telling him
to wait it out.

He had to play it out just a little bit longer.

He remained close to the storefronts, keeping the
windows on his right so he could use the reflections to
watch his back, while still keeping an eye in front of
him.

Then it was time for the coup.

His two-man reception team appeared in front of
him once again. They were about twenty yards away,
drawing his attention, when suddenly Bolan's sub-
conscious sent him a warning signal.

The hit wouldn't come from the two men. They
were just a distraction. It was the man behind them
that he had to watch for.

Lumbering down the street, a head taller than those
around him, was a copper-skinned giant with long
black hair. He wore a thin denim jacket over a faded
work shirt, and torn jeans.

A "derelict."

At least that's what the cover story would be if they needed a fall guy to pin Bolan's murder on.

The giant parted through the milling crowd of men and women with a swift and sure gait. Though he was unkempt and his face masked by the stubble of a beard, he was in perfect shape. Too perfect, too tightly focused on Bolan to be a derelict.

But it was good cover.

The man would strike at the American tourist out of the blue, and the papers would have another tragic mugging to report.

There would be no loose ends. The man was either totally owned by the outfit, a specialist who would be spirited out of the area, or else he would be a contract killer who would collect his money and move on.

The man looked right at Bolan, his coal-black eyes etching a bull's-eye on the American.

Like magnets, both men proceeded toward each other.

The two Forca Militar operatives in front of the hit man came to a dead stop, forming a barricade beyond which Bolan wouldn't be able to pass. The killer fell in step behind them and reached into his jacket.

His callused hand freed a blade from its sheath.

At the same time Bolan noticed the parade of reflections in the store window to his right.

Two more men were coming up behind him—bluesuited head breakers. They slowed to Bolan's pace. When the time came they would hold him or push him forward into the man with the knife.

It would take a few seconds, and everyone would vanish while he slumped to the ground.

The knife came out in the open for a split second, but then the man shielded the blade beneath his jacket.

Five feet from the warrior, the assassin showed the blade again.

Bolan could see the man's strong square teeth shining, glistening in a deadly smile as his hand tightened around the dagger's hilt.

The Executioner looked into the man's eyes, and in them he saw death. But not his own.

There was a slight coughing sound, then the man's eyes went dark.

He sank slowly to the ground as though he were melting. His knees buckled, and he toppled forward, a neat bloody-red hole in his heart.

Bolan stepped forward, a few inches ahead of the hands that grabbed for him from behind and missed, then turned slightly.

The suppressed pistol coughed twice more, and two men in suits went down. One with a hole drilled in his forehead, one with a brand-new bleeding metal ulcer in his side.

With an almost quizzical look on his face, Bolan looked around him—just like the other pedestrians who were amazed to see men dropping dead all around them. And as the warrior looked around, he fired from the hip again.

A triburst took out the fat man in front of him. Another headshot claimed his partner.

The two-man crew who'd been gloating earlier, looking forward to payback time, were cashiered for good. Their unguided bodies fell dead to the ground.

The blood of Forca Militar stained the streets of Manaus.

In the confusion Bolan sprinted ahead, getting caught up in the fleeing passersby and the suddenly shouting window-shoppers. Tourists and terrorists alike were carried along in the crush of the crowd.

Bolan manufactured the same expression of wonder and fear that colored their faces. And like them he shook his head at the unexpected burst of violence that shattered the peaceful afternoon.

And like them, he walked away from it all, the silenced hush puppy quiet and secure beneath the raincoat that had protected him from the sudden squall of terror.

## 10

The strong humid breath of the Amazon River breezed through the villas on the outskirts of Manaus where the houses edged against the jungle. Ornate tiled walkways hung like necklaces around the grand mansions that were as lush as the rain forest. Ponds, gardens and statues studded the grounds of the high-priced homes.

It was the very lushness that bothered Mack Bolan as he rolled the Jeep to a stop at the apex of a cobblestoned driveway, parking just in front of a late-model Lincoln.

The drive looped in front of a tree-shrouded old-world-style manor. A carefully landscaped tree wall screened the gray buttressed manse from the access road.

There was a lot of money behind this safehouse, Bolan thought. Maybe too much. This one smacked of wealth unbounded, the kind of wealth Forca Militar could draw upon.

But he knew from the beginning that Joaquim Almeiros needed heavy backing to play the game he played. The place obviously belonged to one of his influential sponsors.

Besides, if he didn't trust Almeiros, he wouldn't be there now. He rapped twice on the heavy wooden door, then stepped off to the right.

A few moments later the oval door opened and the somber brown face of Joaquim Almeiros appeared. And unknown to him, his face was clearly in the telescopic sight of the .308 sniper rifle wielded by Bolan's backup man concealed in the trees on the right flank.

Almeiros banished the gloomy countenance with a tired smile, genuine warmth flooding his face as he stepped into the shaded bluestone porch and shook Bolan's hand. "I knew you would come."

"No thanks to the welcoming committee that met me in your place a couple of days ago."

Almeiros nodded. "I was called away by a last-minute emergency. So they said. A few of our esteemed bureaucrats suddenly had need of my services—just as I was about to leave for the airport from the training center. It was all nonsense. I was, as you would call it, shanghaied."

"I'd call it a lot worse."

"It was meant to teach me a lesson about cooperation," Almeiros said. "I've been working too hard, they said. Becoming obsessed. Perhaps it would be better for everyone if I concentrated on other things than Forca Militar, which, according to them, is little more than a pipe dream."

"More like a pipe bomb," Bolan replied.

"Yes. I heard about the fireworks." The Brazilian walked over to the side of the porch, standing in a patch of sunlight while he idly scanned the trees. "You were meant to be part of the lesson. Made an example of. After your death I imagine they would have made another approach to me and offered one more chance to go along with them. But fortunately you made an example of them."

"A few of them, yeah," Bolan said. "But we both know there's a lot more out there. Maybe it's time we compared notes. I've got a list of names, outfits and corporations from the Forca Militar people we turned in Jamaica. They mean nothing to me, but to you..."

"Let's go inside where we can talk without feeling under the gun."

Bolan smiled. The man either saw or sensed that Jacques was out there covering him. "I brought a friend along."

"The same friend who picked you up at the airport?"

"The same," the warrior replied.

"Good friend to have."

"Yeah. Just so you and your people know he's with me."

"Oh, we know. We've been watching him ever since the two of you reconned this place yesterday."

"Looks like you've got good people, too."

"Good enough to stay alive this long. Believe me, Mike, down here that's one hell of an accomplishment."

He followed the Brazilian counterintelligence man inside the manor. Despite the grand appearance on the outside, inside was sparsely decorated. A long table with several charts occupied a room to the right of the hallway. And by the window stood a man with a rifle that most likely had been trained on Bolan while he was outside.

But now his rifle was at rest.

The rifleman returned Bolan's nod.

Then Almeiros and the Executioner sat at the long table.

Bolan clasped his hands together and leaned onto the table. "Like I said, there's a lot to go over, but before I go into detail, I think most of it can be summed up in two words—Antonio Moura."

The Brazilian special forces colonel repeated the name, as if it were the password of a secret society. "You and I think alike," he said. "The name has come up more times than I care to count. Every time there is an outrage, Antonio Moura is connected to it. Every rock I look under, I find traces of him. Until now I didn't have the capacity to go after him. Now I have the manpower, the necessary backing from necessary people. But he too has similar backing. Perhaps even more than we wish to think. And I want to tell you one thing, Mike. There is no longer a chance of walking away from this. Either he goes, or we go."

"That's why I'm here," Bolan said. He began to unreel the intelligence that turned up from the Forca Militar insider they'd captured in Jamaica. Cristobal

Cavaros's bodyguard and right-hand man, Jorge, had revealed several sites in the Amazon, staging bases, caches, and cutouts in the military and industrial community that permitted them to conduct their business.

Almeiros confirmed much of the intelligence and discarded the rest, labeling it as guesswork or misinformation that had been fed to Cavaros and his people. But there was enough hard intel that coincided with his own for them to act upon.

And there on the table full of the latest and most accurate maps of the Amazon region the two men mapped out their campaign.

While a river breeze swam through the open windows, carrying with it the heavy, steamy tropical scent, the two men prepared to go to war.

THAT NIGHT, one hundred miles west of Manaus at a remote army outpost in the heart of the Amazon basin, the war came to Project Talon.

The special forces support station clinging to the side of the murky stream was, according to the skeleton crew, just two steps away from hell.

There, at the swampy site infested with insects and a constant dampness from the ever-present rain, waited a small cadre of soldiers who'd long ago earned their Jaguar patches from Colonel Almeiros at the jungle warfare training center based in Manaus.

The Project Talon troops were looking forward to the jungle sweep. They too shared the convictions of

Almeiros, and were tired of closing their eyes to Forca Militar operations.

At last the blinders were coming off.

Colonel Almeiros had been setting up several similar outposts along the Amazon tributaries, using helicopters and riverine patrol boats to reach deep into the inaccessible areas.

They were ready to go to war, but they weren't ready for the war to come to them.

A silent war.

As soundless as the breath that propelled it, the poison-tipped dart pierced the neck of the sentry on duty. His right hand slapped at the needle-thin wound.

It was instinct and habit that triggered the simple motion, like that of a man swatting away a blood-sucking insect.

But the thing that stuck into his neck wasn't drawing blood, nor was it alive. By the time the realization dawned, a crippling burst of heart-stopping poison had short-circuited his system.

His insides seemed to crystallize, then the camou-clad veteran slumped against the wide tree trunk that served as the halfway mark of his rounds, reaching for the thick buttress vine snaking upward.

But his hand never made it.

Statuelike, he keeled over. With a sound like softly falling rain, the dead man's limbs embraced the underbrush.

On the waterfront side of the camp another sentry met his death at nearly the same time. He was sitting in the shadows of the dock, watching the rhythmic rise and fall of the outboards moored there when he heard a hissing sound rift through the air to his left.

Then he too felt the sting of death.

He slumped forward, seeming to fall in slow motion toward the damp wood, his head about to strike hard—until a quick hand lashed out of the darkness and caught the back of his collar, holding him up just long enough for the deathly drug to do its work.

Then the deadweight was lowered to the earth without making a sound.

There was a sudden rush then, like a wind blowing in from the river. Quiet and surefooted marauders cut through the brush surrounding the support base.

The outpost of barracks, cook house and storage sheds had been erected by nearby villagers, fishermen and Brazilian soldiers. It was a staging area, nothing more. No attack was expected. After all, the Jaguars were the ones supposed to do the attacking.

The outposts had sufficient stocks of fuel, food and ordnance to support Joaquim Almeiros's jungle strike force. But despite its isolation, it had attracted fishermen and some of the wandering Indians in the area. Fishermen, farmers and cattle ranchers had already begun trading with the soldiers, welcoming their presence.

But the presence was too much for Forca Militar to bear.

In the eyes of the underground army, the outpost gave Almeiros too much influence in *their* territory.

From the base Almeiros's strike teams could move far and wide into the rain forest, tracking the routes used by FM couriers and convoys.

There was another reason why such a presence had to be dealt with. Forca Militar had been hit hard, in Marajó, in the Caribbean and in the streets of Manaus itself.

Unless Forca Militar responded, the weight of their cowardice would hang them in the eyes of those who feared and obeyed them. And worse, unless a victory came soon, the shadow cabinet that ran Força Militar activities for Martin Machado would call not for Antonio's impeachment, but for his head on a stake.

And so Antonio Moura made his diplomatic visit to the Amazon base of Colonel Joaquim Almeiros in the dead of night.

The Ambassador stood in front of the sleeping barracks. He no longer looked like a patient statesman. Now, waving his automatic rifle, he gave the signal to the rest of the Indians and FM assassins.

They stepped up to the barracks in a quiet and quick motion and assumed a deadly stance.

With a nod of his head, Moura gave the final order. A deafening barrage of automatic gunfire ripped through the thin wooden walls of the barracks, tearing jagged holes and scorching splinters out of the wood. Like men putting out a fire, they hosed the rifle barrels in jagged patterns, stitching every level with 9 mm lead.

Screams thundered from the inside of the barracks, punctuated by the thrashing of trapped dying men as they tried to hurl themselves out of the line of fire.

One man clattered outside the front door and slammed it halfway off its hinges. Clutching his unbuttoned khaki trousers around his waist, he came to a dead stop, jerking from left to right in puppetlike panic, his wild eyes assaulted by the sight of Moura's hardmen coolly strafing the barracks.

It was only a brief glimpse.

A moment later a razor-edged machete sliced through the humid air, then through the soldier's neck. Wielded by the muscled arm of a man who'd chopped his way through the jungle for half his lifetime, the sword decapitated the man in one clean blow.

Then the crew charged into the barracks, the staccato bursts of autofire finishing off the survivors of the initial blast.

While the last sounds of gunfire were dying away, a tall and heavy villager who'd been recruited as a cook for the unit stepped from the neighboring shack. The man was a *cablaco,* one of the countless river wanderers of European and Indian stock who worked and fished, then moved on.

Now, under the eyes of the guns, he realized he'd moved on to the wrong spot and began to plead for his life in panicked tones.

But his voice grew calmer as he saw Moura nodding his head in sympathy with his plight.

"Yes," Moura said, "there are many good reasons why you should go free."

The cook looked warily at the assassins who stepped out from the barracks, most of them splattered with blood. They formed a half circle behind their leader and waited for his cue.

"Thank you," the cook said, bobbing his head. "It is all a sad mistake. I should be home now, I will be going home now... And you can be sure that I...I... Do not worry about what I've seen—I haven't seen anything."

Moura stepped forward. He reached up and put his hand on the cook's shoulder, nodding in tandem like the ultimate politician putting his constituent at ease.

"Many, many reasons why you should return to your people unharmed," he continued, soothing the man.

The cook smiled, revealing bad teeth that spoke of a hard life.

"Except one reason."

Moura's long slender fingers darted to the man's throat and squeezed hard, knuckles whitening as he pushed his prey back against the house, slamming the man into the wall.

With each slam he increased the tension of his grip, but his voice stayed calm and conversational as he explained to the pinioned man why he had to die. "You see, the people in the area, our good friends, they all must know what happens to those who collaborate with the enemy."

The dying man leaned forward, his face turning blue, his tongue protruding and eye rolling while the ambassador of Forca Militar said with some sympathy in his voice, "These things are necessary."

**11**

Three twin-engined AS 355 Ecureuil helicopters droned above the rain forest canopy, a lush illusory carpet of green that looked solid enough to walk on.

As the lead jungle-camouflaged chopper neared the support station, the pilot dropped low for a stealthy approach, painting the Ecureuil's rippling silhouette large upon the treetop carpet.

The other two helicopters followed suit, then began to move forward in a leapfrog pattern, one scout protected by two backup gunships who then alternated taking the lead.

Door gunners scanned the forest below, their hands on pintle-mounted FN 7.62 mm machine guns. The choppers also had fixed twin 7.62 mm pods for forward firing and a variety of 70 mm rockets and 20 mm guns—enough to pour a lot of hellfire on the enemy below, if the enemy was still around.

Bartolome Marquez took the lead for the final approach to the landing zone. He knew the route blindfolded. The support camps and villages used by the Brazilian special forces were permanently imprinted in his mind—as permanent as anything could be in this ever-changing part of the Amazon.

The rotor wash stirred up an angry tribe of chittering monkeys and brightly colored long-beaked birds as Marquez flew just above the hurtling green ocean of forest.

Sitting up front across from the pilot was Joaquim Almeiros. The commander was somber, his normally expressive face cast in a deathly mask beneath the high-tech helmet, a slender wraparound mike protruding from the side like an electronic appendage.

"Try again," he ordered.

Marquez nodded, then radioed the support base. No luck. He tried a few more times before turning to Almeiros. "Nothing."

"It's bad, as bad as we thought," Almeiros said, voicing the suspicion that had been growing in his mind ever since the trio of choppers took off from the Manaus base. He lapsed into silence then, and stared out at the rain forest.

When there had been no reply from the support base earlier in the day, everyone had feared the worst and hoped for the best. The jungle base had a powerful radio. The weather was clear. If they could speak, they could have checked in. And now, if they were able, they would have responded.

When word about the deafening silence reached Joaquim Almeiros, he abruptly ended a meeting with a top-ranked internal security man who was going to run surveillance on the corporate arm of Forca Militar.

"Maybe they had to move out quick," Marquez ventured.

"Maybe they sprouted wings and flew into the sun," Almeiros bit out, sitting back in the cockpit chair and massaging his eyes, the kneading motion producing a burst of images on the inside of his eyelids. Points of light like spirits, he thought.

"It could have been a flood," the pilot said, though his voice lacked conviction. "Or maybe a fire. There could be many reasons they had to go."

"They're still there."

"How do you know?"

"I can hear them," Almeiros said.

"But the radio—"

The colonel shook his head. "The dead have low voices, but they make themselves known."

The pilot looked straight ahead, not about to argue the point. He was used to the cloak of mysticism that Almeiros sometimes shrouded himself with. It wasn't uncommon in any section of Brazil, whether metropolis or jungle, for civilized men to carry such unusual beliefs around with them. Even in the military, perhaps especially in the military, superstition, magic and religion were alive and doing well.

Catholicism, macumba, candomblé, shamanism and half a dozen other religions collided in Brazil, blending into a strange and heady mix that provided a bewildering, enchanting pantheon of gods and god-desses for the faithful to follow.

Many of Almeiros's commandos shared some of his beliefs. It was impossible not to. After all, he was the man who forged them into this covert unit—a shadow outfit within an already-secret force. He was the man their lives depended upon.

The Jaguar patch he and his men wore was part logo, part totem. A fitting emblem, the jaguar was a black and deadly creature of the night. Seldom seen, his presence was always felt. The same could be said of Almeiros's small cadre.

This supernatural esprit de corps didn't harm his performance in any way. When it came to combat, he was down-to-earth. And when it came to hunches, he was often right.

Mystic or madman, Bartolome Marquez would hate to have the Jaguar chieftain on his trail. He'd seen him in action too many times to doubt Almeiros's hunting skills. Like the jaguar, once he selected his prey there was little that could stop him.

Marquez glanced sideways, saw Almeiros sighing, steeling himself for the sight he would soon encoun-ter.

It would be a miracle if anyone was alive, Marquez thought as he banked for the final descent to the clearing by the riverbank.

Then he saw that there would be no miracles.

A fire had destroyed the barracks area, reducing it to ashes, a funeral pyre for the bodies within. Broken boards and collapsed walls had spread out onto the ground, leaving a shadow of ash around the bodies.

The two other helicopters passed on the left and right, soaring above the green-carpeted corridors with door gunners peering at the forest below.

Like a scythe cutting through grass, the rotor blades of the lead chopper sent up a storm of brush and leaf-green debris as it dropped toward the ground.

The sliding doors on both sides of the chopper rolled open and several soldiers in forest green fatigues and flak vests pushed off from the compact benches, preparing to disembark.

One of them was Mack Bolan.

As the chopper descended, he cradled the M-16 A-2 that had been issued to him. Each man in the Project Talon strike force also carried a .357 Smith & Wesson revolver, several grenades and either an Uru or INA subgun.

For firepower Bolan stuck with the M-16 and a .357 revolver. Well versed in their use, it was all he needed to jump into action.

But the time for action had passed, the Executioner thought.

Any hopes of rescue were quickly dashed as the commandos stared at the devastated outpost. Though they were ready to descend upon the overrun jungle encampment, they had little hope of finding anyone alive.

Only ghosts awaited them in the forest below.

Still, experience had taught them that unless they wanted to risk joining the ghosts, they had to treat this as a potentially hostile zone.

The Executioner hit the ground running. He moved off to the right, keeping an eye on the edge of forest that crept up to the settlement.

The other commandos fanned out through the silent outpost while the two other helicopters circled overhead, ready to lay down covering fire with a bristling array of weaponry.

But the only live targets on the ground were the commandos who quickly secured the zone.

The members of the strike force were little more than undertakers, Bolan thought, there to count the dead, spirit them away, then try to catch those who were responsible.

The first chopper lifted off, making room for the other two, which in turn landed to drop off more of Almeiros's troops. They spread out into the surrounding jungle, looking for casualties, survivors, a witness.

The sentries were found where they were slain, like grisly sculptures still standing guard after they'd passed on.

Almeiros walked around the barracks like a man in a trance and spoke the name of each man softly, giving a last farewell to those who went to their death because they were loyal to him.

Loyalty was a two-way street. And it didn't end here.

That was clear from the purposeful strides Joaquim Almeiros made around the death site, looking every last man in the face, or what remained of him, seeing how he died.

It appeared that most of them were dead before their ambushers torched the barracks, but there was no way of telling if any of the bullet-ridden bodies had held on to life while Forca Militar washed them in flame.

"I will not forget you," Almeiros stated fervently.

Bolan surveyed the carnage, stopping at the civilian who'd obviously been strangled to death, his carcass spared from the fire.

"This one wasn't a soldier," the warrior observed.

"No," Almeiros agreed. "Just another survivor—until now. He came in to help us. To help himself. The wages he was paid could make life easier for his family. Not much, but enough to keep them in food for a season."

"It's obvious he wasn't a soldier, but Forca Militar killed him."

"It is their way," Almeiros replied. "They send a message to us and to people who might think of helping us."

"We've got to send a stronger message."

"As soon as we find the animals who did this," Almeiros said.

But "soon" could be a lifetime, Bolan thought. He had little hope they would close in very quickly on the

Forca Militar contingent that carried out the massacre.

Not in this wilderness.

The secluded location, though ideal for supporting in-country probes, was also its greatest weakness. Built alongside one of the hundreds of Amazon tributaries that coursed into the interior, the support base was in another world. It was the hub of a hundred different escape routes.

Forca Militar could vanish in any direction, just like they could strike from any direction. They operated in the cities, on the rivers, deep in the rain forest, blending in wherever they went.

In the funereal gloom of the camp, the soldiers moved quietly from body to body, wrapping them for the return trip to Manaus. One chopper would stay in the area, scouting. Two would carry back the bodies.

"We bring in the troops, they fade away," Almeiros said. "We hit them, they hit us. And the war goes on with no decisive victory. Sound familiar?"

Bolan nodded, thinking of another jungle in another era where war was fought under arbitrary rules. Certain areas were off-limits from attack, so that was where the enemy holed up between battles. And here it was almost the same. The leaders of Forca Militar operated in the jungles, then retreated back to their high-rise headquarters in the cities, a boundary line where they were protected from men like Almeiros.

So they thought.

From the look on the commando leader's face, Bolan knew he was ready to cross over that line.

Jungle or high rise, it was all the same to him now. He was ready to attack.

And so was the Executioner. He caught a whisper of movement at the edge of his vision. It was just a slight shifting of fronds that could have been waving in the breeze.

He tightened the grip on his M-16 and turned casually toward the source of surreptitious motion. Gradually his eyes discerned a human shape among the trees. It moved though, as soon as his eyes had picked it out.

"We're being watched," Bolan said.

Almeiros nodded, raising an eyebrow in a congratulatory gesture. "Most people don't see him until it's too late. Don't worry, he's one of our assets. We have mutual interests."

"I wasn't worried for myself," Bolan replied, still aiming his rifle toward the intruder.

The Brazilian waved to the man in the forest.

A moment later a tall, light-skinned Indian stepped into the open. He planted a thick brown long bow into the ground, holding it like a staff at his side. Red dyes decorated his lean body in an elaborate pattern from head to toe. His muscles were corded and pronounced, just like the vines snaking through the jungle around him.

As Bolan moved closer to Almeiros he could make out the shape of the painted marks. They were paws with sharp claws. The tracks ran up and down his body, totem markings, Bolan realized, identifying the Amazon warrior with the spirit of the animal selected as his hunting or warring god.

The markings were a reminder that at any time the man could become the creature.

He wore a red loincloth and had a long machete strapped at his side. Dark leather armbands stretched across his biceps, and a necklace of sharp fangs hung around his neck.

"I don't recognize the uniform," Bolan said.

"Jaguar," Almeiros said. "Just like us. In fact, that's one of the reasons he first came to us. When he saw our Jaguar patches he figured we might be after the same prey."

"Or worshipped the same god," Bolan said, aware of Almeiros's animistic beliefs.

"That too."

When the two men approached the Indian, other figures moved in the forest, cloaking their motions with the natural swaying of the thick green bush. They came near enough to the edge of the woods to see and be seen. They, too, had markings similar to the first warrior, but not as numerous. Clearly he was the leader.

Almeiros introduced the Indian as Haraya, an approximation of the warrior's name in his native tongue.

He and the warriors behind him were Yanomami Indians.

Almeiros spoke to the Yanomami chieftain in a mixture of rapid Portuguese and the native Yanomami dialect. He spoke to him as an equal, as if Haraya and his handful of men were the Army of the North and he and his Project Talon were the Army of the South.

From time to time the Indian warrior looked at Bolan while Almeiros spoke.

Finally the Brazilian colonel turned to Bolan and briefed him on the Yanomami presence. Messengers from one of Almeiros's other bases called upon their Yanomami allies in the area to scout for the Forca Militar party and rendezvous with Almeiros here at this base.

"We have electronic surveillance from the choppers above," Almeiros said. "But even more accurate, we have surveillance from the Yanomami below."

This band of warriors were refugees from their lands to the north. The wild region between the Amazon River and the Venezuelan border had long been the traditional hunting grounds of the Yanomami— until recent years the largest group of aboriginals untouched by modern man.

Their way of life was coming to an end. There were still hundreds of villages and small clusters of Yanomami, but clandestine gold-mining operations launched by Venezuelan and Brazilian freebooters had staked their claim to their area. And more than once those stakes were right into the heart of the Indians who already lived there.

Reaping most of the benefits of the gold rush was Forca Militar, preying on the mining camps, stealing or buying the precious ore at cut-rate prices. Those who refused to deal with them them didn't keep on breathing.

And those who stood in their way were pushed out. Like Haraya's clan.

"I see how they can help us," Bolan said. "If they stay in touch with the rest of the tribes, that kind of network can zero in on Forca Militar bases. But can we trust him?"

Almeiros laughed.

"What's so funny?"

"He asked the same about you."

Bolan smiled. "Good question to ask. You got any answers?"

"Yes," Almeiros said. "On both counts. Haraya lost his family to a Forca Militar raiding party while he was out hunting. His children were killed, their heads dashed against rocks. His wife was taken by the guerrillas to provide entertainment. They used her for three days before killing her. Haraya found her hanging upside down, gutted and practically drained of her blood."

The Brazilian nodded toward the other warriors. "Their families met similar fates. That's why they're here and why they work with us. They know we chase the same enemy. That's why we can trust them."

Bolan looked at Haraya.

Though they were cultures apart, there was a strong connection between them. Both warriors had lost their families to the same murdering breed. Evil lived in the cities, and it lived in the Amazon. And wherever it dwelt it had to be hunted, had to be crushed. To do that took another kind of breed, men like the Executioner. Men like Haraya.

Bolan stepped forward, looking the Yanomami chieftain right in the eyes. He saw a light gleaming in those dark eyes, which were almost mirror images of his own.

"Tell him we are of the same tribe," Bolan said. "The lost ones. I know the pain that lives inside him."

"I suspected as much," Almeiros replied. "There had to be a reason why you stuck it out this long and why you were so willing to come this far." He spoke to Haraya, repeating what Bolan had said and adding a few words of his own.

The Indian warrior's hand came straight out, open palm, open fingers. Bolan stepped closer, mimicking the gesture and then clasping hands.

Haraya had an iron grip and an iron heart. He had nothing to live for but war.

"I'm glad he accepts you."

"Why's that?"

The Brazilian lowered his voice and said, "That blade of his isn't just for decoration. Around here we call him Harry the Headhunter. Anyone who isn't with us just might end up in his collection."

**12**

The gold camp was a splintery ruin. Wreckage littered the riverbank. The long wooden sluices that washed riverbed deposits through burlap screens, separating gold from sand, had been tipped over and smashed. Pickaxes used to crush rocks into smaller pieces were sticking high in the trees around the camp where they'd been flung.

Acrid chemical odors drifted across the remnants of the makeshift camp that had been discreetly perched on a northern sliver of the Amazon that branched out into the lush and previously unspoiled region. Chemicals used to heat and bond the gold had leached the soil where the containers had been dumped. Gasoline fumes from the shattered pumps that ran the sluices hung in the air.

Green-tarped shacks and supply sheds with camouflage-painted zinc roofs had been smashed, the twisted pieces of metal and broken boards scattered around. Sacks of rice and beans were torn open on the ground.

There was no sign of life in the camp. The survivors had fled.

Only two men remained behind. One of them, the chief negotiator for the miners, had been buried alive. The Yanomami Indian who'd worked with him for the past two years was killed almost as an afterthought, shot in the back of the head.

The miner's most current name was Roberto. Like many of the marginals and prospectors in the area, he'd accumulated a lot of names in a lot of cities, leaving aliases behind when he fled into the Amazon to scrape a living from the earth. He had a reputation as a man of honor in the mining community, though his past was clouded with arrests and his future would have been dim if he had fallen into the hands of the law.

Falling into the hands of Forca Militar proved worse.

They'd marched him to the bottom of a ten-foot man-made cliff that the miners had previously dug out from the riverbank to get at the richer deposits.

The site was already dangerous when the miners had abandoned it and worked their way farther down the riverbank. Their progress was marked by a series of artificial gorges hacked out of the riverbank by pick and shovel.

When Roberto stood at the base of the tilting embankment, the Forca Militar gunmen forced him to keep digging until the dangerously angled cliff began to slide.

After a subtle rainfall of sand and pebbles trickled down the cliff, there was a tearing and wrenching sound followed by a rumbling growl. The yawning earth exhaled a rush of air as it collapsed around the miner.

Now Roberto was entombed in a ten-foot wall of rock and clay, his grave marked by the corpse of the Yanomami Indian who stood by him.

The miners and the handful of Yanomami Indians who lived near the camp, hunting wild game for them in exchange for carbines and alcohol, stood silently by while the camp's negotiator met his fate. No one was foolish enough to confront one of Forca Militar's roving death squads in the open.

And in a way it had been expected.

Somehow Forca Militar had found out that the miners were holding back nearly half of the ore they'd pried from the ground, stashing away the larger nuggets they found and selling them to other traders at higher prices than Forca Militar offered.

No doubt an informant in the camp figured secrets such as that one were as good as gold and sold his information to the guerrillas.

The Forca Militar flotilla of high-powered boats had made its way up the river to the mining camp in broad daylight, and armed men had leaped ashore before most of the miners knew what was going on. Some men managed to flee into the woods, but most of them were rounded up to watch the speedy trial and even quicker executions.

Every ounce of gold in the camp was appropriated by the guerrillas. They left the rest of the miners alone, penniless witnesses who would spread the tale of what happened to those who tried to deceive Forca Militar.

Word of the raid swept quickly through the riverside mining communities.

And word spread through the Yanomami grapevine that the Forca Militar locusts had struck once again.

The Indians couldn't win.

The land was no longer theirs. Either mining operations bankrolled by Forca Militar came into their territory and pushed them out, or Forca Militar took over independent operations where the miners got along with the Yanomami.

Either way the result was the same—the tribes were heading for extinction. They were on their way out unless they fought their way back in.

That's why they made sure word of the latest Forca Militar assault reached Haraya, the Yanomami who'd befriended the Jaguars.

COLONEL ALMEIROS REACHED the site two days after Forca Militar had turned it into a ghost town.

He arrived with a riverine force of a fast patrol boat, two six-man airboats with 350-horsepower engines and caged aircraft propellers, and a trio of long narrow dugout canoes powered by small outboard motors. Each dugout carried a contingent of warriors from Haraya's clan.

Above them came the unmistakable sound of helicopter rotors carving a path through the pungent air.

The Ecureuil choppers were back in action, no longer on graveyard duty.

The troops were massing at the abandoned mining camp. The base was a perfect staging area for the raiding party of special forces men and Yanomami warriors.

There was a deathly serious mood about them, Bolan thought, an attitude he'd run into countless times before. It wasn't going to be just another temporary show of force, a halfhearted army patrol going through the motions.

This time there was no doubt as to where the enemy was located. The Forca Militar raiders who had hit the mining camp were based near a string of ranches upriver, well-known to the miners and the Yanomami who'd tracked them there.

It was the territory of Pedro Luna, one of Antonio Moura's top enforcers. Luna was the current ranking "diplomat" for Forca Militar, a man who considered this stretch of river his province where law was a chimera that existed only in his mind. Murder. Robbery. Rape. Slavery. It was all the same to him. All in a day's work.

Soon he would run into one of the rare occupational hazards, Joaquim Almeiros.

**13**

Waves rocked the yacht gently, splashing steadily against the gleaming white hull of the nincty-three-footer cruising the shoreline of the wide stretch of Amazon known as Rio Negro.

Like a million-dollar lure, the yacht had attracted the cream of the crop of models and debutantes from Manaus who'd eagerly signed on for another one of Antonio Moura's expeditions.

The destination was nowhere in particular. Getting there was all the fun.

The yacht had long ago left behind the bright lights of the capital's skyline, high-rise steel-and-glass stalagmites that speared the night.

Earlier in the evening at the marina, a steady parade of glittering and giggling deckhands had boarded the yacht. Masked woman with jewels and pearls diving into abundant fields of cleavage came aboard in clinging gowns, wraparound shawls and swimsuits that were more whimsy than fabric.

They were the ones who would make sure it was a pleasure cruise. Just one more reward for Moura's hardworking crew. They took risks, so they reaped the appropriate rewards.

Music streamed from slim, glossy black speakers spread around the "rec room," a teak-and-leather-lined stateroom that had been converted into a world-class bar and ballroom.

At the moment there were five other men in the room, attended to by a clinging coterie of women who looked like goddesses. But in their intoxicated state the men, despite their well-tailored clothes, looked like bandits.

Such things were necessary, Moura thought.

Just like the Old Man of the Mountains had given his Hashishim followers a glimpse of heaven before sending them off to battle and rewarding them with even more glimpses if they survived, Moura gave his men a taste of the good life whenever he could.

It was usually just a brief respite from the other world they lived in—the world of violence.

A well-stacked redhead with green eyes drifted to Moura's side. The floor-shaking music swallowed most of her words, but at the end he heard her say something about wanting a tour.

She cocked her head, birdlike, a beautiful creature of prey with bright plumage. A volcano of red hair splashed down onto her bare shoulders. Her black gown overflowed with well-tanned breasts, and her eyes twinkled behind a black Vienna mask with lace trim and glittering spangles.

An actress with small success, large assets, auditioning for a part in his life.

"What did you say?" Moura asked.

"I asked for a tour, Antonio," she repeated. Her glossy red lips parted in a teasing pout. "Show me around?"

"I'll draw a map if you like," he suggested. "That way you can see for yourself."

"That's only half the fun. Besides, there are a few things I could show you."

"Ten years ago, perhaps," he said. "These days I'm not so sure."

"Antonio," she scolded him, "there's only one way to find out."

"You're a girl after my own heart."

"Among other things." She smiled, sliding her fingertips down the lapel of his silk jacket. Then she curled her fingers around his hand. "Come on, Antonio."

He broke free of her soft grasp. "In a while, Gina. Go. I'll catch up to you. But first there are some matters I must attend to."

She laughed, assured that she was culled from the herd. His for the night. Maybe longer.

The music and the smoke and the clinking of glasses blended into one sound. Now and then a shouted name, shrill laughter and decadent moans punctuated the chaos.

Such things were necessary, he reminded himself as he left the stateroom and climbed up onto the deck.

Cool tropical air wafted against him as the yacht headed upriver.

The air was intoxicating. So was the high-powered hull that sliced through the water.

That was his pleasure—the power, the speed and the wealth that he commanded.

But mostly it was the power, which soon he would have to demonstrate.

In addition to the crew two other men were on board, associates of Forca Militar who thought lately that they were heads of their own organizations. An illusion Moura had to break.

Antonio walked to the wheelhouse, then stepped into the brightly lighted haven. He leaned on the darkly burnished wood console and looked out through the glass at the darkness. "Take us out," he ordered to the pilot.

"How far?"

"Far enough so a man couldn't swim to shore," Moura replied. "If he was so inclined."

The pilot nodded, then turned the wheel without saying a word and took them on a course toward the middle of the river.

It was several miles wide at that spot. Even a superman might think twice about risking the current. And the man he was dealing with wasn't quite a superman. Perhaps in a boardroom he could hold his own, but here? Moura thought. No. This was Forca Militar's floating turf.

He went below deck to one of the cabins where Eduardo Quayone, respected Manaus businessman, waited with his personal bodyguard. And with a Forca Militar gunman.

As soon as the Ambassador opened the door, Quayone's spindle-thin body leapt from his chair. His normally somber face was stretched with a phony smile.

His bodyguard, a clean-shaved man who was perfectly groomed, stood beside him with his hands folded in front of him. He looked confident and brave, refined, the type of unobtrusive bodyguard a prosperous businessman wouldn't be embarrassed to be seen with in public.

Refined but wrong for the job, Moura thought. The man was smart enough to accompany his high-paying boss, but dumb enough to have no fear. It still hadn't occurred to him what kind of situation he had placed his boss in.

"Antonio," the silver-haired businessman said. "So glad to see you. We have been waiting quite some time."

"Yes."

The other man looked uncomfortable. "I thought you wanted to discuss the, eh, potential deal."

"I thought I asked you to come alone," Moura said, looking down at him and ignoring the bodyguard who suddenly seemed alert and was now leaning forward.

"Of course," Quayone said. "But who goes anywhere alone these days? I thought it would be safer—"

"You don't think I can look after your safety here? On my very own boat?"

"It's not that. You see, he is more of a friend than protection for me—"

"Good. Then your *friend* can stay here while you and I go talk privately."

The bodyguard started to protest. But then Moura nodded toward the Forca Militar hardman who'd been leaning against the wall, silently watching them. "He can stay with my *friend.*"

Quayone welcomed the chance to save face. "Fair enough."

A few minutes later they stood on the side deck, looking down at the dark waters of the Amazon rushing by. Muted music played in the background.

"Now we can talk," Moura said. "But first..." He reached inside his jacket, then began patting the empty pocket. "How foolish of me. I left my cigarettes below. Excuse me, I'll be right back."

"Have one of mine," Quayone suggested.

"No. It has to be my brand. I'm a creature of habit."

Moura pushed open the door to the cabin without knocking, smiling when both bodyguards stood at attention.

"I forgot something," he said, looking from one man to the other. "Relax. I am here only for cigarettes. All you have to protect me from are my own bad habits."

Quayone's bodyguard laughed politely.

Then his teeth clacked together like a porcelain hammer.

The fist that crashed into the underside of his jaw was a levered blur. Moura hadn't even changed his pace as he walked past the man and hit him with the right uppercut.

The motion tilted the bodyguard's head up just as Moura's left hand cocked back at the elbow. His bunched fist rocketed forward and caught his target right beneath the nostrils with rigid cartilage-busting knuckles.

There was a loud crack and an explosion of blood.

As the bodyguard crumpled, Moura grabbed the back of the man's collar and flung him headfirst into the opposite wall. Streams of blood raced down the wall to the carpet.

Discarding the bodyguard, Moura grabbed a cigarette from the Forca Militar hardman, whose eyes were wide with admiration. Only a few seconds had passed.

"One moment," the guard said, gently tugging at the left sleeve of Moura's jacket. "There is blood."

"Oh." He turned slightly while his gun-toting valet removed the jacket for him.

"HOPE I DIDN'T keep you waiting," Moura said when he returned to the side deck, cigarette in hand.

"Not at all."

"Good. Now at last we can talk."

Moura did most of the talking.

Eduardo Quayone was a longtime associate of Forca Militar. The businessman had frequently been on the receiving end of the guerrilla group's largesse. Forca Militar provided the money to set up legitimate factories in the duty-free port. The legitimate factories provided the hardware and the machine-tooling technicians necessary to set up the clandestine arms factory that supplied Forca Militar and its ever-growing clientele. And Quayone took his cut.

He oversaw the entire operation of the Midnight Arms manufacturing runs, producing high-quality knockoffs of sophisticated weaponry. They always selected models that could be made cheaply with stamped metal parts and sold expensively to those who wanted reliable but untraceable weaponry.

It all went well.

Until now.

Quayone was getting too cautious. He felt he was being watched and thought the law was closing in on him.

"We are the law," Moura said. "Or we can buy the law if we need it. That's what Silva does. He is so high up in the security apparatus that he can fix anything that comes along. You have nothing to worry about . . . from the law."

Moura's voice and his eyes said there was plenty to worry about from him, however.

The slender businessman looked too vulnerable now, the Forca Militar liaison thought. Like a twig, he could be snapped, discarded. There was no challenge. No sport.

How easy it was to break a man's will, to twist him around until he recognized who controlled his fate.

"It is too dangerous to go ahead with the operation. We should hold off until the heat passes."

"Is that your best advice," Moura challenged.

"It is best for everyone that way. Keep everyone in the dark. Make no waves."

"You know what I think, Eduardo?"

"What?"

"I think you're quick to take the money, but slow to pay the price."

"What do you mean?"

"When the money first came in and there was little danger, we heard no complaints. Now, when we require your aid, you wish to forget your debt to us."

Quayone pressed against the railing and looked down at the blackish waters. He had no argument.

"There are risks in everything," Moura went on. "That is how nations are built and fortunes are made. That is how we maintain our territories. How we *must* maintain them. And that is why your talk of a 'potential' transfer is so offensive. It is not potential. It is actual. It must go ahead. You will supply us with the weapons as we agreed."

"But I'm telling you I'm being watched!"

Moura shrugged. "That's only natural. Your kind should always be watched."

Quayone bristled. To no effect. Moura ignored his anger and mocked his fear. So the man was being watched. It would come to nothing. Forca Militar had people to take care of such problems. Of course there was always the possibility that the man would be used as a scapegoat, his body given over to the authorities. He would make a perfect sacrifice. Forca Militar would rid itself of an unwilling ally, and the authorities could claim their latest crusade a victory. And then another clandestine arms factory would be set up.

"It is too risky," Quayone pressed.

"No more than usual."

"Our opinions differ too much. That is why I wish to contact the, eh, man at the top in Rio and explain the situation to him personally."

Moura laughed. "Machado! You wish to contact Martin Machado and yet you cannot bring yourself to even mention his name?"

The other man bowed his head.

"Go ahead," Moura goaded. "Say it."

"Martin Machado."

"There. See? No lightning bolt struck you. You are still alive even though you mentioned his unholy name."

"I have to talk to him," Quayone repeated. "There is no other way."

"A moment ago, my friend, you talked of risks. Let me explain about Machado. If you go outside the regular channels to contact him, it is not a risk, it is a certainty that your throat will soon be cut."

Quayone shook his head. "Then *you* must listen to reason. If we go ahead with the production and delivery of the weapons, it will all come down on our heads. But if we postpone matters for just a little while—"

"Tell that to our friends in the SNLA."

"Why them?"

"They are the ones depending on us for this shipment." Moura enjoyed the look that appeared on Quayone's face at the mention of the guerrilla army. In neighboring Suriname the government was fighting a long-running battle against the Suriname National Liberation Army, a.k.a. the Jungle Commandos, one of several resistance groups provided by Forca Militar.

"How can I talk to them?"

"Very simple," Moura replied. "I'll take you there myself." He pointed toward the jungle-shrouded northern shore of the river. "We can meet with one of their representatives at any time. And then all you have to do is explain that you are feeling a bit timid, a bit wary and they'll have to carry on without the weapons we promised them. I'm sure they'll understand."

"No. It is not my field of expertise. I'll leave that to you."

"Of course. But you know there is still another way."

The slender man looked up at Moura, suddenly wary of any of the Ambassador's suggestions.

"Aren't you curious?" he asked.

The other man shook his head.

Moura dropped his hand on the man's shoulder and ushered him toward the rear of the yacht. The lightweight businessman offered negligible resistance, practically skipping on his toes to keep up.

The Forca Militar ambassador grabbed the back of Quayone's neck and squeezed hard, forcing him to look over the rail, straight down into the churning wake of the yacht.

He twisted his neck left, then right. "The shore is far away, Eduardo. If you want to get off, fine, get off here. Leave us now, and you'll never have to worry about us again."

Quayone pushed back but was unable to gain any leverage against the Ambassador's iron grip.

Moura suddenly released his hold.

The man tumbled backward, losing his balance and collapsing in an ungraceful heap onto the deck.

"This is no way to treat *me!*" the businessman shouted, pushing himself off the deck.

"It is but one of many." His voice was suddenly smooth and friendly. "Come, let me show you another." He gestured for the underground armorer to follow him below deck.

A few moments later they stepped inside the cabin where Quayone's bodyguard waited for him.

"Oh my God," he said, looking at the trail of blood stretching from the wall to the floor, where the unconscious man was sprawled out.

"Relax. He's not dead—though that could be easily arranged."

Quayone was speechless, his eyes filling with fear.

"You do see the writing on the wall? You do understand?"

He nodded.

"Good," Moura said, ushering him out of the cabin. "Now that our business is settled, let us go and enjoy ourselves."

**14**

The cluster of men in jungle-green camous gathered at the eastern perimeter of Pedro Luna's land, safely harbored in the night-black shadows of the thickly canopied rain forest.

The Jaguar commandos carried an impressive array of armament—sniper rifles with night-vision scopes, flares, M-16 A-2s with M-203 grenade launchers attached.

Equally well armed were the Amazon warriors who waited impatiently beside them for the word to attack. Their faces were painted and their long curved blades were honed to head-severing sharpness. They were ready for close-quarter combat or, with their long bows, long-distance fighting.

Earlier a team of Yanomami warriors had helped provide security for the sapper team Bolan led to the T-shaped junction at the north end of the long driveway that led from Luna's bastion to the potholed dirt road.

The Executioner had positioned a string of Claymore mines to cut off anyone who tried to escape in the vehicles that were parked alongside the house, mostly Jeeps and Blazers with outsize tires, and a small-bladed bulldozer.

Such hardy vehicles were necessary for survival in this wild country. Though the Brazilian government had once tried to connect much of the Amazon interior with dirt highways, many of those ambitious projects had been abandoned after floods and the creeping rain forest ate away the roads.

Small access roads that led to the often-impassable dirt highways had to be maintained by the people who used them.

Hence the heavy vehicles.

The mines were embedded in the dirt embankment at the junction of the drive and the access road. The long snakelike detonating wire was carefully hidden in the brush, ready to spew its steel venom.

The land forces alone were strong enough to hit Luna's stronghold, but Colonel Almeiros was taking no chances. A riverside fleet waited out of sight, ready to sweep down on the southern perimeter where half a dozen boats waited at Luna's dock.

The third force at Almeiros's command was the trio of flying gunships standing by.

"Remember," Colonel Almeiros said. "I want Luna alive if possible. But I don't want you dead trying to take him in. If he survives the first attack and we can take him, fine. But if it comes down to it, if there's any doubt about your safety at any time, smoke his ass."

The commandos nodded.

Bolan went along with it. He, too, wanted the Brazilian Forca Militar diplomat alive. Luna had a hand in just about every operation of the underground army. According to Almeiros's intelligence, Luna was the one in charge of the surviving American prisoners. Several Yanomami had also seen gaunt white men working on Luna's vast holdings.

Such a man could help them a good deal. But only if they were alive to act on the intelligence, which was why Almeiros had spent so much time lining up the assault. He believed in giving the enemy a chance. Not much of one, but a chance just the same.

After the shock of the initial attack, the Forca Militar garrison inside Luna's jungle fortress would have an opportunity to see how outgunned they were.

One of the Jaguar commandos carried a portable backpack loudspeaker that Almeiros would use to make his demands to the guerrillas. His plan was simple. Hit first, talk later. If the talk didn't produce results, hit again.

The Brazilian counterinsurgency specialist had mapped out just about every stage of the battle, covering a number of different scenarios they might encounter.

Such detailed planning was admirable, Bolan thought. Except for one thing. All those carefully thought-out scenarios could go out the window the moment the shooting started. It was almost impossible to predict how a man would react when he came under attack. A man in an impossible position often did impossible things. The Executioner had been in that situation often enough, from both sides, to know that every man was a possible berserker when death stared him in the face.

Crouching beneath a stand of thick fronds, the warrior raised the hand-held night-vision device one more time and scanned the killing zone. Through the thermal imager he could see the length of the block-house-shaped stronghold, most of its windows dim. Then he focused on the lone sentry, a man he would soon view through another scope—one with cross hairs.

After the quiet kill, the others would move into position, and then the house of Luna would fall.

So he hoped.

THE OBSERVATION POST for Luna's stronghold was a deck on top of a first-floor extension that jutted toward the driveway. The rectangular crow's nest offered a clear view of the wide driveway that bisected the tall grassy land.

A heavily armed guard was sitting in the crow's nest in a slanted wooden chaise longue that was too short for his long legs. The man's firepower was impressive. His side holster held a .357 Magnum, and he had an automatic rifle with a stick magazine resting across his lap. But the firepower impressed only himself. Not the men who watched him from a distance.

Bolan had moved to a rise that gave him a clear line of fire into the crow's nest. A blanket of foliage surrounded him on all sides as he dug into the damp earth, viewing the sentry through the scope mounted on the Accuracy International sniper rifle.

Beside him Almeiros and two of his Jaguars also studied the fortress through night scopes.

So far only one guard had been seen.

Forca Militar was confident in its ability to handle anything that came at them, perhaps relying too much on their savage reputation to entertain the thought that anyone would dare to hit them.

That reputation was about to be shredded by the Jaguars concealed in the brush.

Once the sentry was silenced, the commandos and Yanomami warriors would move forward, leapfrogging toward the blockhouse.

Through the scope the Executioner watched the man who would soon give ghostly testimony to the fury of Project Talon. The sentry was watching the stars, not the grounds. His left hand dangled idly at his side, his right hand draped over the stock of his automatic rifle.

The only thing he was really on guard against was his own people. Now and then he looked toward the door that led from the deck to the second-floor entrance. A couple of times he had pushed himself off the chair and stood at attention, as if he heard voices or footsteps from the doorway. Both times he'd been satisfied they were false alarms and sat back down again.

Finally someone was approaching.

The sentry stubbed out his cigarette on the floorboards and leaped to his feet. Then he glanced out at the rain forest, his rifle at the ready, looking like a fierce sentinel, a noble Forca Militar guardian. A few moments later a man stood on the threshold, admitting a sliver of light before closing the door behind him.

He wore a pair of ragged cutoff shorts, and a T-shirt stretched across a massive chest and an even larger gut. He also held a large brown bottle in his hand, one of several that no doubt had contributed to his beer gut.

He exchanged a few words with the guard, then went back inside the house.

The guard stood at attention for another few minutes, listening carefully to the other man's departure. When he was satisfied the man was gone for good, the sentry resumed his previous position and sprawled out in the chaise longue.

"Give me the word whenever you're ready," Almeiros said, "and I'll call in the choppers." He raised the slim transceiver that kept him in touch with the Ecureuil gunships.

Bolan zeroed in on the sentry's forehead. "I'm ready."

The Brazilian commando chief raised the lead chopper on the transceiver. "We're going in," he said to the pilot.

Then he turned to Bolan. "Take him."

The Executioner inhaled, then let his breath out slowly as he squeezed the trigger.

There was a soft cough as the 7.62 mm round sped toward its target.

Like an eggshell cracking open, the front of the sentry's head shattered. The stars he'd been watching for so long suddenly went out, and his lifeless body slumped back against the chair.

Bolan moved the barrel of the rifle slightly to the left and focused on the doorway in case anyone had heard a sound and was coming to investigate.

But the door remained closed.

The fate of Forca Militar was sealed.

"Let's move," Almeiros said.

With a sudden rustling, like a deadly breeze, the Yanomami warriors moved forward. Their bare feet silently rushed over the ground, avoiding the vines that snaked around the property.

After reaching halfway to the house, the warriors stopped.

The second wave moved on then, almost as silent. Just as they'd envisioned all the time they'd waited, Bolan and the Jaguar commandos covered the ground without a misstep. Then they dropped down in the tall grass while the Yanomami moved again.

Finally the combined ground force was close enough to the house to move all at once. If they were detected now, they would open up with everything they had. But with the sentry silenced forever, there was little chance of that.

A small group of Yanomami Indians and commandos headed toward the woods at the end of the driveway junction while the rest of the force closed in.

The dark crouching shapes cut furrows through the tall grass as they steadily moved forward. Then the two-story blockhouse loomed before them.

Bolan came to a stop at a clump of brush that looked down on the southern edge of the house from a distance of forty yards. "Any closer and we'll trip over them."

Almeiros nodded and checked the position of his men. "This is it," he said. "Get ready to knock on the door."

Bolan pumped a round into the M-203 low-velocity grenade launcher and sighted on a roofless gray Jeep with a roll bar that was parked a few steps away from the entrance facing the waterfront.

One of Almeiros's flak-jacketed commandos on the northern side of the house sighted his M-203 on the other entrance.

"Fire," Almeiros ordered.

Bolan squeezed the trigger, launching a 40 mm high-explosive grenade into the side of the Jeep. The blast rippled metal and plastic into the air, ripping off the windshield frame and hurtling shattered glass against the house.

Like an instant echo, another grenade hit the opposite side of the house at the same time.

A dozen riflemen fired up at the house at a slanting angle, strafing the windows and wood with automatic bursts, intentionally firing high to avoid random killing. They wanted to smoke out Luna, not incinerate him.

The clatter and chaos grew into a loud, endless barrage as smoke and tear-gas grenades thumped through the broken windows. An HE airburst grenade chomped a hole in the middle of the roof, sprouting tongues of flame that licked up at the sky.

Above the tumult came the loud, droning sound of three choppers homing in on the now blazing battlefield.

The fast patrol boat and several dugouts came into play now, strafing the dock and unloading more commandos onto the shoreline.

PEDRO LUNA HURTLED down the second-floor hallway of the house, shirttails flapping behind him, waving the Ingram MAC-10 he'd snatched from his bedside table when all hell broke loose.

All around him men were shouting, footsteps were pounding down the halls and stars were shining down through the splintery holes of the shattered roof.

He called out to the men who were quartered on the second floor, but in the madness few could listen. And those who saw him raving like a maniac in his underwear and unbuttoned shirt were not inclined to follow his instructions at a time like this.

Luna had never been in a pitched battle before. At least not one pitched entirely at him.

The Forca Militar diplomat ran halfway down the stairs until a series of white-hot explosions ripped through the windows. In the flash of the stun grenades, he saw his disoriented men running around in panic. Some of them stood rooted to the spot, as if they wanted first-row seats at the apocalypse.

He turned back upstairs and headed toward the second-floor deck with a group of his men. They burst out onto the deck, some of them holding their submachine guns over the side and firing off wild, unaimed bursts.

Well-aimed return fire cut down two of his hardmen as soon as they reached the railing. Two others screamed in agony, dropping their weapons and stepping back with blood flowing from their chests, their hands clutching at the arrows that had rippled through their flesh and sent them reeling backward.

The controlled slaughter sent the rest of Luna's men running for cover, some of them jumping off into the darkness, others rushing back inside, a step behind Luna.

Luna started screaming in rage—at Antonio Moura for leaving him in charge while the Ambassador was in Manaus; at the men who were falling around him, and at the army that was hitting them with everything they had. Finally he screamed at the god he'd long ago abandoned.

The conscience that had lain hidden all these years was coming to the surface once again, the conscience that promised him all along that retribution would come.

A STREAM OF GUERRILLAS flowed down the side of the house, leaping from the second-floor windows and landing on top of an old station wagon that had seen better days.

The survivors were bailing out. The diplomat's once formidable-looking house was now a sinking ship.

Bolan moved closer to the building, flames from the upper reaches flickering wildly, smoke billowing from the bottom floor. He scanned the handful of men who'd jumped ship and saw one of them with a submachine gun rising from his hip. The Executioner triggered a burst that punched the gunner back against the house, his head tumbling through a smashed window, his back catching on the shards of glass.

The warrior fired another burst that ended the man's screams.

The entire line of Project Talon commandos advanced, deadly shadows picking off any Forca Militar gunmen who offered resistance.

Somehow in the confusion two guerrillas piled into one of the Jeeps that was parked between two other ATVs. The driver slammed the vehicle into reverse, and with a loud groan and thump the car behind it was pushed away. Then with a screech of tires and a spray of dirt, the Jeep careened down the driveway and smashed through the wooden gates, sending them spinning in the air like twigs. Then it turned to the right.

As the driver cranked the wheel, a commando depressed the Claymore detonator. Steel shredded the Jeep and blasted into the gas tank. The vehicle spun end over end, then blew, sending the gunmen down a far different road than the one they'd hoped to travel.

Back at the blockhouse, bright spotlights encircled the flaming structure as the whirring, droning copters descended to the ground, door gunners sweeping the rooftops with covering fire.

The choppers made one pass, then banked away from the house, keeping it lit up as bright as day.

Then all firing stopped.

Almeiros's voice boomed into the night, using the backpack loudspeaker to call for their surrender.

The sudden quiet worked miracles.

Moments ago, the men inside the house had been dodging lead and crumbling beams as their world came down around them. Now they were given a chance to walk out.

And they took it.

In ones and twos the guerrillas climbed from the windows and jumped from the gaping holes where the doorways used to be. As soon as they touched the ground, they were thrown facedown in the dirt by the commandos, who held them in place with hot metal barrels at their heads.

"Where is Luna?" Almeiros shouted.

"Over here!" answered one of his men, who'd dragged a survivor away from part of the house that was aflame.

The Brazilian commando chief ran over to the wounded man, reaching him just a few feet ahead of the Executioner who stared down coldly at the diplomat.

Pedro Luna was hysterical, crying and screaming. With good reason. The right side of his face was covered with blood, his shirt was scorched and there was a large splinter of wood sticking into his arm like a spear.

Almeiros pointed his M-16 toward the man and squeezed the trigger. The burst of autofire silenced him. The bullets had eaten into the dirt just a couple of inches from his face.

"This is not the time for tears," Almeiros told his prisoner. "And we are the last people on earth who would care."

Luna managed to gather himself into a sitting position, drifting into another stage of shock. In just a matter of minutes his whole world had been turned upside down, and standing before him was a man who might bring that world to an end.

"What do you want?"

"I want Antonio Moura. I want Forca Militar. I want you and your people to pay for every drop of blood you've shed."

"*Yes!*" Luna said, clasping his bloodied hands together in front of him like a man making a confession. "I can talk to you. I can explain it all…" He saw his out, a way to escape the bullets that had been flying all around him. "If you don't kill me."

"What you tell us now determines if you live," Almeiros said. "Or how you will die."

He nodded dumbly.

"First give me Antonio Moura."

"Moura," Luna said, spitting out the name. "The great Ambassador. He is in Manaus. He is on his yacht while I sit here bleeding and burning. He's cruising with his whores while I do all his work for him."

Colonel Almeiros listened, guiding the babbling man's confession. He was in the perfect frame of mind to reveal everything he knew about Moura, but it came forward in a jumble of names and places, all of it spoken with intense hatred, like a man choking on vomit. He still couldn't see that he was responsible for the path he'd taken, preferring to blame it all on someone else.

"Enough for now," Almeiros said, looking at the man in black beside him. "This man also has a question for you. Speak to him as you would to me. If you hold anything back, you are a dead man."

Through his dazed eyes, he sought out the face of the Executioner.

"What is it?" Luna asked.

"The Americans. Where are they?"

Luna laughed hysterically. "I knew it. The Americans. The scarecrows. That's what brought this on our heads. We should have killed them long ago but—"

Bolan's right cross caught him squarely on the jaw. Luna dropped back on the ground.

The Executioner leaned over him and grabbed the lapels of the guerrilla's shirt, raising him halfway off the ground. "I don't want your feelings," he growled. "I want to know where you're holding those men."

"They're at one of our ranches," Luna replied. "Not far from here."

"How many?"

"Two."

"There were supposed to be five," Bolan said.

"Three of them died from their wounds."

Bolan's cold eyes pinned the man to the ground. "From battle, or were they shot afterward?"

Luna hesitated.

The warrior slowly and deliberately slapped a fresh magazine into the M-16, dropping the barrel until it was pointed at the middle of Luna's head.

"The truth, guy. That's all that separates you from the three Americans who died. Unless you want to join them right now, you better tell me all about it."

Luna was flat on the ground, spread-eagle, like a martyr for his cause. "Two of them died from wounds. The other one..."

"Keep talking."

"The other one was shot in the head."

"Who did it?"

"The Ambassador."

"'Ambassador,'" Bolan repeated. "High-minded sentiments for a murdering bunch of bastards. Ambassador and diplomat.'' He glanced at Almeiros and saw that the Brazilian was regarding the guerrilla with the same kind of scorn. Noble names, ignoble deeds.

"All right," Bolan said. "Take us to the Americans."

Luna nodded, then forced himself to sit up. One of Almeiros's men helped him to his feet. Though he was groggy he was able to walk. The wounds weren't critical, just painful.

And there was a strange kind of glow in his eyes, almost one of eagerness. They were the eyes of a man who'd just talked his way out of a death sentence.

"Welcome back to the living," Bolan said. "As long as you were telling the truth, that is."

"The truth," Luna agreed.

About five minutes later Almeiros and the Executioner boarded the nearest Ecureuil with their prisoner.

The chopper lifted off, accompanied by another aircraft as it flew toward the ranch where the Americans were being held, following the glittering black ribbon of the Amazon for twenty miles.

Both choppers circled the ranch before selecting a flat stretch of ground for a suitable landing zone. Then, in the blaze of light provided by both choppers, the lead chopper settled down near a ramshackle hut.

When the second chopper landed, a squad of commandos jumped out and took up positions between the helicopters and the main ranch house, which now showed lights in several windows.

Bolan pushed Luna out of the chopper and marched him toward the hut, which was barred from the outside.

"Open it," the warrior ordered.

Luna fumbled with the long wooden crossbar but finally managed to remove it. He threw it on the ground, swung open the door and stepped aside.

A fetid rush of air escaped from within. The hut was little more than a stall filled with straw and stained with human misery. Sweat, blood and tears had left their mark.

Inside the stall were two men, both of them looking like scarecrows in the bright yellow light that beamed from the nearest chopper.

It took a few minutes to awaken the American prisoners. One of them was groggy, delirious, unaware of his surroundings. He was laughing, or maybe crying. It was hard to tell in his present state.

Almeiros and another commando carried him outside to the chopper.

The other American managed to climb to his feet, half aware of what was going on but still staring in disbelief at the man in black who led him outside.

"Who are you?" he asked, his scrawny hand pressed against the door frame for support. His hair was long and unkempt and his eyes were sunken, but a fire still burned within. "Where you from?"

"Mike Belasko," the Executioner replied. "From the U.S.A. I'm a friend, guy, here to take you home."

"Lawrence Adams, sir," the man said. "And I hope to hell this isn't just another dream, because I don't think I can take any more."

"It's no dream," Bolan told him, pointing his thumb at the chopper behind him. "We're getting out of here."

The man took three steps forward before he dropped, catching onto Bolan's shoulder. The Executioner swung the lightweight ex-prisoner off the ground and carried him into the waiting chopper.

**15**

The clandestine armament factory was located on a narrow side street near Mercado Municipal, the huge marketplace that handled most of the fresh fruit and fish that came into Manaus's bustling port.

At night the marketplace was quiet, as were most of the streets surrounding it.

But this night there was plenty of activity inside the factory.

While most of the building was devoted to high-tech workstations that assembled motorcycle frames and gears, the third floor was reserved for more profitable manufacturing.

Black paint shielded the floor-to-ceiling glass windows and skylights. Heavy tarps then masked the windows, preventing light from escaping, and muffling the sound from the late-night assembly runs.

At three in the morning the midnight shift was finishing up, packing away the well-oiled machine pistols and subguns in long wooden crates.

Two forklifts carried stacks of crates to the cargo lifts, their booms rattling and forks digging up sparks from the oil- and grime-soaked floor.

The crates were dropped into the elevators, then lowered to the loading bay on the main floor where they were stacked in front of a corrugated metal door. A few hours later another Forca Militar crew would back the truck to the dock and pick up the deadly cargo.

As they climbed down the stairs from the third floor, only a small skeleton crew remained behind in the huge high-ceilinged factory. And feeling very much like a skeleton was Eduardo Quayone.

Eduardo Quayone dismissed the night workers when everything was in position. The silence of the trusted, secret shift workers had been purchased long ago by the high hazard pay and the threat of sudden death if they talked.

The other members of the crew didn't belong to him.

Down on street level the workers left in twos and threes, filing quietly out of the metal doors on the sides of the buildings.

The other members of the crew didn't belong to him.

Down on street level the workers left in twos and threes, filing quietly out the metal doors on the sides of the buildings.

All under the watchful eye of Colonel Joaquim Almeiros.

When the last workers vanished from the courtyard, Almeiros signaled the black-clad commandos who'd been waiting in the shadows. They moved to the doors, expertly wielding a variety of tools that pried the metal lock wells from the brick foundations. Then they trooped into the darkened factory.

It was time for Project Talon to go to work.

WHEN THE ELEVATOR clanked to life and began its ascent to the top floor, Rogerio Silva frowned at Eduardo Quayone.

"Your people can't even follow orders," the barrel-chested man snapped. "The building was supposed to be cleared."

"My people are dependable," Quayone replied, pushing his chair from behind the long metal desk, standing and staring at his unwelcome guest. "They pay attention to detail. Perhaps there's a problem that needs looking after. You do want the shipment to go out on time, don't you?"

Silva nodded. He'd taken it upon himself to be on the premises tonight to make sure that the wavering Forca Militar frontman followed through with the latest shipment.

Eduardo Quayone had become quite dangerous lately. Gone was the enthusiasm with which he took dirty money for dirty work. In its place was fear.

Such men couldn't be tolerated very long. To maintain its reputation and its position in the underworld, Forca Militar couldn't traffic with questionable allies.

Quayone would be dealt with soon. A few days after the weapons transfer another man would be brought in and familiarized with the operation. And then, shortly after they gave him a huge bonus for his work, Quayone would be taken out.

The noisy elevator clattered past the second floor.

Silva jerked his head at the closed elevator well. His two enforcers moved toward the elevator, Uru submachine guns up and ready. They split up, each man taking one side so they could catch anyone inside the car in a cross fire.

The elevator came to a shuddering halt, and the doors hissed open.

Both Forca Militar gunners stepped forward, poking their gun barrels inside.

"Empty," Silva pronounced as the doors hissed shut again. He looked accusingly at the white-haired businessman who stood there equally dumbfounded. "What's going on here?"

"I have no idea."

"I do," Silva said. "This building is either plagued by ghosts or—"

A loud voice suddenly boomed behind him. "Or by Jaguars. Project Talon Jaguars."

Silva turned and saw Colonel Almeiros, as well as half a dozen other men who had filtered up the rear stairwells, quietly working their way through the third floor while the elevator distracted the enemy.

And he saw the tall man in black, the American he'd faced once before at the airport.

Frozen by the sight of the commandos in night gear, the Forca Militar gunners kept a tight grip on their 9 mm submachine guns. Like men in suspended animation they didn't dare to move, not while the sound-suppressed submachine guns of the Jaguars were drawn to them like magnets.

Quayone looked almost relieved at the interruption. But he was uncertain what to do, his hands nervously pressed to his sides while his eyes slowly moved back and forth from the crooked intelligence man to the Brazilian commando chieftain.

"I see you found each other after all," Silva said to Bolan and Almeiros, his voice full and rich. "Good. There was some mix-up before that I tried to straighten out."

His words hung falsely in the air.

Bolan stepped in his path, putting the corrupt intelligence man between him and the two gunners by the elevator.

"I remember your welcoming committee," the warrior stated. "A reception like that is hard to forget."

Silva shrugged. "A misunderstanding. These things happen in our trade. But everything can be worked out. We all have our needs. Tell me how I can help you."

Though the blatant offer of a bribe fell on deaf ears, Silva continued talking. He spoke as if the lure of wealth were an enchantment that would hold any sane man in its spell if only it was offered long enough and loudly enough. But soon he realized these men weren't sane, not in his worldview. They were immune to corruption.

"Then it seems," Silva said, carefully picking his words, "all I can offer you is—"

He dived backward, a signal for his gunner to shoot. They had no choice. Silva's sudden motion had plunged them into battle whether they wanted it or not.

The Forca Militar gunmen raised their weapons, trying to aim them at the commandos.

But there wasn't enough time. In that split-second interval half a dozen silenced subguns spit out a barrage of 9 mm autofire that drilled both guerrillas where they stood. The impacts of the rounds punched them back against the elevator doors, their unfired weapons clattering to the floor.

At the same time, Almeiros fired a short burst from his silenced weapon, killing the traitorous intelligence man before he hit the ground. He landed with a heavy thud on the dusty floor, his right hand still clasping the side arm he'd attempted to free from its holster.

Quayone stepped forward, hands raised, eyes flicking from man to man, surprised that *he* was still alive. "What do you want?"

"Nothing much," Almeiros said. "We want business to go on as usual—until we close it down for good. We also want the names of all your associates. And we want you to write a statement of your connections to Martin Machado."

"That's like signing a death warrant."

"Perhaps," the colonel replied. "If you would prefer an unsigned death warrant—" he waved the short-barreled suppressed SMG at him "—that too can be arranged."

"What if I cooperate?"

"If you cooperate fully, that will be taken into consideration. A shorter sentence. Protection. Who knows, you might even come out of this a hero. The trapped businessman who helped save his country from a subversive organization. The media needs heroes, they need patriots. And we need someone whose word will stand up once all the smoke clears. Someone from the inside. Someone respected in the business community."

Quayone nodded. "I have always been a patriot. In my own way."

"Of course," Almeiros said, letting him hold on to the illusion. "Then might I suggest that as a patriot, you continue with the shipment. When the Forca Militar truck arrives, give them the weapons. We'll follow the truck to Moura's yacht."

"And then?"

"And then we'll complete our transaction with Forca Militar."

**16**

Two-tiered riverboats were a common sight on the Amazon, threading leisurely courses between the freighter traffic and huge passenger liners that routinely traveled the thousand-mile journey from the Atlantic to Manaus.

Though the two-deck boats were of considerable size, large enough to comfortably sleep thirty or so passengers and crew, they were dwarfed by the massive ships and often had to turn to the shallower sections of the river to avoid collisions that would send them to the bottom.

Most of the two-deck riverboats were used for tourist expeditions, fishing trips and for luxury cruises. Ranging from stripped-down models with thatched roofs up to state-of-the-art luxury boats with sleek fiberglass cabins that hummed with air-conditioning and music, the riverboats never caused much notice.

But the one that shadowed Antonio Moura's yacht drew a lot of attention from the armed crewmen on the rear deck.

Especially at this late hour.

It was approaching midnight, and they were more than fifty miles downriver from Manaus, traveling the brown-water section of the Amazon that got its coffee-tinted color from the merging of the Solimões and Negro rivers.

It was several miles wide, dark and dangerous.

The man leaning forward in the cockpit chair trained his rifle on the bow of the riverboat, trying to acquire a target. For the past few hours he and his fellow sentries had kept a steady eye on the river traffic, ready to open up on any other ship that came near.

So far they'd all been false alarms.

But each boat that appeared on the water had to be checked out.

They all had their tasks. The pilot would bring them to their destination, Antonio Moura would sleep through the long monotonous cruise until they hooked up with the Suriname guerrillas and it was time to oversee the transfer, and men like Luis and Gabriel took their turn on watch.

As the riverboat increased its speed and drew nearer to the yacht, the men on watch finally the saw the figure in the night scope attached to the Heckler & Koch rifle.

He laughed and put down the long-range weapon. This was a figure that deserved a lot more study.

"This requires our complete attention, Gabriel," Luis announced, grabbing the thermal-imaging binoculars they used to scan shorelines to make sure that no unwelcome hosts awaited them in the woods when they made their clandestine landings.

"What is it, Luis?" the other watchman asked, his voice as tired as his body.

"We're on the wrong boat."

"Nothing new there, friend."

Luis zoomed in on the top deck of the riverboat cruising along behind them.

A woman was dancing, encased in a clinging body stocking that revealed a lush figure. "Now that is definitely a pleasure boat," Luis said. "That is where we belong tonight. See for yourself."

Gabriel grabbed the glasses and zeroed in on the late-night spectacle. In the monotonous blackness of the Amazon, such a sight brought him fully awake.

"You're right," he said. "Maybe we should board her."

"Another time. Another place. Tonight the Ambassador has no room for play. Too bad we are on a business trip."

Gabriel nodded, staying focused on the apparition. They had hundreds of miles to travel on the Amazon before they began the second leg of their journey, sailing north up one of the rivers that cut through the wilds of Brazil into the even-wilder jungles of Suriname.

Visions such as this could keep a man's soul alive during the journey.

He stayed focused on the girl until the riverboat fell back as it cruised lazily toward the shore.

FROM THE OUTSIDE it looked as though the occupants of the riverboat were ready for a party. The upper-level rear deck was covered by an awning that protected smooth-contoured benches from rainfall so passengers could enjoy the ride. Multicolored lanterns ringed the front deck, which could double as a sunbather's aerie or a ballroom. The wheelhouse was shielded from the sun with large wraparound glass that gave it a streamlined look.

All in all, to anyone who saw it, the riverboat looked like a self-contained miniature hotel.

Looks could be deceiving.

On the inside, the boat was ready for war. Packed with an arsenal of automatic weapons and night-fighting gear, it was a floating battleship.

The wheelhouse also sported sophisticated communications equipment that enabled it to receive television transmissions from a U.S. Key Hole digitized reconnaissance satellite that Brognola had tasked to the region.

Antonio Moura's yacht had been watched ever since it picked up its cargo of unmarked weapons at a secluded slip north of Manaus. Satellite transmissions revealed the makeup of the crew, all Forca Militar hardmen, and the course it was following.

The riverboat was well ahead of them before the yacht began its downriver trek. To throw off suspicion of pursuit, the riverboat left Manaus several hours before the yacht, letting Moura's flagship catch up and pass them.

There was little danger of losing track of the yacht.

According to intelligence they'd plucked from Quayone, the latest shipment of weapons was destined to end up in the arms of a liberation group in Suriname. That meant the yacht would most likely follow the Amazon downriver until it could turn north at either the Erepecurú or Parú.

But first it had to get past the men gathered in a double-wide cabin on the lower deck of the sleek white riverboat. Shielded from the hot river air and prying eyes, the group of American and Brazilian commandos sat waiting to go into action.

Cool clean air hissed into the room from the air-conditioning ducts. For most of the trek downriver they'd been quiet, each man mentally preparing himself for what was to come.

As the time passed slowly by, they lived out the engagement in their minds, visualizing themselves walking away from it when it was over. That was the most important armor, the psychic shield that let them place themselves under fire. The belief that they would prevail.

By now every man on board was ready to close in on Moura's yacht, ready for war with the Amazon Army.

So was the woman on the upper deck.

The "dancer" with long brown hair and long sun-browned legs, who moved in abandon to the music, looked like expensive talent for expensive tastes.

But she was much more substantial than the full-figured fantasy role she was playing tonight. She'd spent years in the Company, earning her spurs as a covert operator in Europe. She'd used her looks and assumed a waiflike persona to infiltrate terrorist cells in Lisbon and Portugal. To the wealthy egocentric leaders of the burgeoning terrorist cadres, she appeared to be the perfect type of follower—beauty and no brains, someone who could be used.

But she was also someone who knew how to use *them*.

Once she was on the inside she destroyed them, demonstrating a ruthlessness and a proficiency with weapons they would have admired—if only they'd survived their encounter with her.

The other Americans aboard the chartered boat were equally talented, capable of posing as local crewman or cruising tourists, whatever role Jacques required them to play.

Jacques had carefully assembled the team when Brognola first sent him into the area with a blank check and an open-ended order to back up the Executioner's operation.

As midnight approached, that operation was about to begin in earnest.

Mack Bolan checked his weapon one more time.

"It's not too late to back out," Almeiros said. "It's my duty, my responsibility, to get Moura. You don't have to go through with this."

Bolan looked straight at the Brazilian counterinsurgency specialist. "Yeah," Bolan replied, "I do.

Before we freed the prisoners I told you I'd stick with you to the end. And after we freed them, I'm still telling you the same thing."

The two Americans were being cared for in a well-guarded hospital room in Manaus. An official from the American consulate would be on hand for the duration.

Almeiros had arranged for the ex-hostages to be tended by top military doctors that he personally trusted. As soon as they were in good enough shape to be moved, the Americans would be transported back to the States on a chartered flight from Manaus to Miami.

"Believe me," Almeiros said. "I'm not trying to convince you to abort the mission. I just want you to know I understand the sacrifice you and your people are making by staying down here. All of you could leave right now and forget about these madmen. You could make this a real pleasure cruise. Just like that." He snapped his fingers.

"Forget it. Moura is here, Colonel, and we've got the right craft to hit him with. We've already gone over that. A patrol boat would scare him off. So would choppers. He'd head for shore, abandon ship and he'd just walk away from this.

Bolan shook his head, then said, "No, the Ambassador's got debts to pay. And we're here to collect."

"As you wish. You know the risks. But you are more than welcome. I just wish to let you know that you can call off the operation."

Bolan shook his head.

"It's already on."

## 17

Mack Bolan sat on the swivel-backed chair on the forward deck and watched the dwindling lights of the Forca Militar yacht bob up and down in the water ahead of them.

The riverboat moved in tandem, rocking and swaying in the swift-moving current. It had been falling in and out of view of the yacht all night.

Now they were the only two boats hurtling down this stretch of water. The last lights they'd seen onshore had been from some pinpoint camp fires at a small village a couple of miles back. This isolated stretch of water was the perfect killing zone.

For either side.

Here the Amazon was a dark raging corridor that flowed between heavily forested shorelines on both sides. At times the visibility had been low, but now grayish clouds above were moving fast, splintered by steady winds and streaks of moonlight that played upon the rushing waters.

For the past several miles the Forca Militar yacht had been angling closer to the northern shore while the riverboat slowly adjusted its own course and headed for an interception without making it too obvious.

Bolan leaned forward and adjusted the binocular eyepiece of the Barr and Stroud IR18 Thermal Imager with its NOD/A passive long-range sight. The large 120 mm eye relief of the swivel-mounted unit offered a wide glimpse of the target without straining his eye.

The Executioner scanned the shoreline, then swiveled the long-range unit back to the yacht. He zeroed in on the name splashed in elegant script across the stern of the yacht—*Cálice*.

Then he sighted on the pair of Forca Militar gunners who had fallen into a semitrance, lulled by the hypnotic roar of the motor and the river.

"Any signs of activity?" Almeiros asked.

"No more than before," Bolan replied. "The crew and the gunners are just marking time."

Almeiros nodded. "They probably won't be expecting any potential trouble until they meet up with their customers near Suriname. Then they'll be fully on guard. Despite their high-minded talk of causes and brotherhood, there's damn little honor among these thieves."

"Don't worry," Bolan said. "The *Chalice* won't get that far."

Almeiros laughed.

"What's the joke?"

"The joke, my friend, is the name of the yacht. Do you think Antonio Moura is a holy man who would name his boat after a sacred vessel?"

Bolan shrugged. "My Portuguese isn't the best—"

"True."

The Executioner smiled. One of the reasons Almeiros preferred speaking in English was Bolan's limited knowledge of Brazil's national language. "But as far as I know," he said, "the *Cálice* means 'chalice.'"

"In English, yes. But if you think and speak in Portuguese, then *cálice* sounds just like *cale se*. And that means, 'silence'!"

That was more in keeping with Moura's philosophy, Bolan thought. The man's business depended on silence and secrecy. And the lives of the people in Forca Militar depended on their ability to keep those secrets.

A few moments later Jacques climbed up the stairwell. "The latest satellite transmission just came in."

"And?" Bolan prompted.

"We're looking at our best window of opportunity so far. If we move in now, we shouldn't run into any other traffic."

"This is your ship, Jacques," Bolan said. "If you think we can do it, then let's climb though the window."

Luis WOKE UP with a start, practically falling out of the bench seat he'd been napping on.

The guerrilla gunman was still clinging to the shreds of the dream that was dissolving inside him, and his heart beat frantically.

"What the hell—" he said, his hand reflexively clutching the rifle he'd slept beside. He raised his head up and looked toward the source of the commotion.

It took a moment for his eyes to decipher the multicolored image floating toward him.

Gabriel also woke up from his slumber, sitting across from Luis at the other end of the long bench on the rear deck. Like a pair of groggy bookends come to life, they both uncoiled their stiff limbs and glared at the floating carnival.

Green and red floodlights shone down on the upper deck of the riverboat, once again illuminating the stunning brown-haired woman. But now the riverboat was much closer. They didn't need to spy on her through glasses.

Her hips were moving slowing to the African and Brazilian rhythms that seeped from the loudspeakers and floated clearly across the waters.

Snake charmer, Luis thought. He couldn't take his eyes away from the ravishing sight.

"Her again!" Gabriel said. "It can't be. I was just talking to her a moment ago in my sleep. She must have heard me dreaming."

"Dreaming?" Luis said. "It was your turn to keep awake. My turn to catch some sleep."

"Both of us should have stayed awake, Luis," Gabriel responded. "And with a fine woman like that, I would have no trouble staying awake."

The woman of their dreams waved to them as the riverboat drew closer. It was still behind them a bit, running a parallel course starboard, about fifty yards away.

"She's saying something," Luis said.

"I can't hear her."

"Try keeping your mouth shut."

The woman's voice carried across the water. It was loud but lilting, as seductive as the music that enveloped her gyrating body.

"She wants to come on our yacht," Luis said. "This is horrible. She's drunk. She's crazy. She's beautiful. And we can't have her. Why tonight? Why does it have to be tonight?"

Gabriel suddenly looked thoughtful. "Yes. Why tonight?"

Luis glanced at his fellow watchman. Then he slapped him on the shoulder. "You are afraid of her?"

"It's just—"

"It's just nothing," Luis said. "Nothing at all. But if you really are suspicious . . ." He raised his rifle and used it to return the girl's wave.

It had no effect on her.

She was still shouting to come over. These days in Brazil a rifle was a common sight. Especially in the untamed regions of the Amazon.

Just then a crewman from the wheelhouse hurried to the rear deck. "What the hell is going on?" he said. "How could you let them get so close?"

"How could you not?" Luis asked. "Look at her yourself."

The crewman cursed. "Get rid of her before this racket wakes up Antonio. Or before I wake him up." The crewman stood by, dividing his anger between the woman on the riverboat and the two gunners.

Both men suddenly grew somber. They shouted at the woman to go away. She shouted back, still laughing, still beckoning.

As THE RIVERBOAT closed in on the yacht, the Executioner and the rest of the rifle team were crouched behind the solid railing that circled the side deck.

The position gave them the high ground to shoot down at the yacht. There was another tactical advantage on the side deck. Jacques had buttressed the railing with hard-faced armor plating. The shield wall was packed with enough ceramic reinforced plastics to protect it from armor-piercing fire.

Like the music that pounded from the speakers on the foredeck, the rifle team was ready to rock and roll.

"STOP!" LUIS SHOUTED. "Go back."

The woman's response was drowned in the music, but it was obvious she wasn't going anywhere.

Luis shook his head, then he shook his fist at her.

She still waved back.

"Something's wrong," Gabriel said, stepping behind Luis and flicking a selector of his Heckler & Koch G-3 to the full-auto position.

"Don't get crazy, Gabriel."

"Not crazy," he replied, raising his voice to yell above the music that grew louder as the riverboat approached. "There's no one else on deck there. Where the hell are they?"

"Cool down," Luis soothed. "It's just a woman."

"Won't be the first one we banged," Gabriel said, slowly stepping to the side and raising the Heckler & Koch, which was loaded with a 20-round box magazine.

"I'm telling you," Luis said. "It's under control."

"The hell it is," the crewman replied, reaching for his automatic pistol. "This boat shouldn't be here. Figure it out. Lights. Music. The bitch is a lure. No one else in sight. It's a setup."

"He's right," Gabriel said.

"Just wait a bit," Luis pleaded. "Until we're sure. Look at her! She's still waving to us. She doesn't know what she's doing."

"Neither do you," the crewman said. "We can't take any more chances. Fuck her. Fuck the crew. I say we kill her, then do the whole fucking boat. Just to be safe."

"Give it some time—"

"There is no more time," the crewman said. He raised his hand, wielding a short-barreled black 9 mm automatic that slowly bore down on the brown-haired dancer.

Then the gun jumped clear in the air, along with a chunk of flesh and bone torn from the crewman's wrist. Blood spouted from the shattered stump at the end of his arm as he staggered back in agony. He stared in disbelief at the side deck of the riverboat where the yellow flashes of autofire had erupted.

The victims had turned victorious.

While he was still adjusting to his own personal Armageddon, another burst of gunfire roared from the riverboat. The lead barrage kicked the crewman over the side, dead before he splashed into the water.

As though hellhounds were snapping at his heels, Luis turned and ran. He lost his balance and hit the deck in a sprawling dive that slid him out of the line of fire. He kept on going, crawling, running, shouting in panic every step of the way.

Gabriel stayed behind, hypnotized for a fatal few seconds by the sudden eruption of fire. He was unable to trigger his Heckler & Koch because of the lightning bolts that had just speared his chest.

And in his dying moments he saw the woman wave one more time. But this time at the end of the wave, she opened her hand and released the grenade that had been concealed in her fist.

The high-explosive bomb burst into the cockpit, shredding metal and splintering the floorboards where Gabriel's dead body had just landed.

The riverboat rifle team strafed the yacht in a concentrated sweep that chewed holes into metal and plastic, seared through wheelhouse glass and severed the mast of the *Cálice's* flag, which snapped in the wind.

From the lower deck of the riverboat two men with 12-gauge shotguns fired StarFlash Muzzle Blast shells, pouring incandescent streams of blinding light onto the yacht just as Forca Militar gunners arrived on deck.

The directional stun grenades held the gunners in suspended animation. Bathed in the unearthly candlepower of the brilliant light, they could only fire their guns blindly, burning off full clips of automatic fire that stitched the darkness with flame. The sound of the jagged barrage was more frightening than its effect. Most of the bullet sprays shot straight up in the air like fireworks. Still under the concussive spell of the StarFlash stream, the Forca Militar gunners were unable to pick out their targets.

But their targets could see them.

Bolan leveled his M-16 and swept the deck of the guerrilla gunboat with controlled 3-round bursts.

Two guerrillas were killed immediately, doubling over as if they'd been hit with a giant unseen hammer.

A third gunner danced backward across the bow, his arms flailing over his head and his weapon spinning end over end like a baton in the air. He stared down at the gouts of blood erupting from his body. And then the awkward dance ended as one foot stepped on thin air and he vanished overboard.

Colonel Almeiros stood beside Bolan, firing short precise bursts that thinned the guerrilla ranks even more.

It was the same all along the side deck as the rifle team poured lead into the yacht.

There was no room for sympathy here. The Forca Militar gunmen were all stone killers, psychopathic marauders finally meeting the fate that was due them years ago. And that fate came down in a relentless curtain of lead.

The battle stations on the riverboat had been carefully thought out beforehand. The pilot in the wheelhouse matched speed with the Forca Militar yacht, staying close enough to turn it into a floating shooting gallery.

The objective was to overpower the yacht before it had a chance to try evasive action.

It was accomplished with stunning effect.

While the rifle team on the upper deck pinned down the guerrillas, Jacques commanded a second unit on the main deck that unleashed even heavier ordnance.

Wielding an Armsel Striker automatic shotgun with the metal stock folded on top, Jacques fired from the hip, triggering a 3-second burst that emptied the 12-round drum and tore through metal and bone on the boat opposite. One of the gunmen on the yacht had turned toward the shotgunner but before he could take aim, the pilot light in his head was extinguished by a skull-shearing shotgun load.

Though it sounded like a cannon going off, the Armsel Striker had twin pistol grips for balance, and there was hardly any recoil. Jacques lowered the heavy-duty deck sweeper and picked up his automatic rifle once again.

Men standing on both sides of Jacques poured a different kind of fire onto the ship, thumping incendiary grenades fore and aft. White phosphorus burst against the *Cálice*'s hull and deck, igniting the air and coating the yacht with a wall of flame.

It looked like a Viking funeral ship. But there were still men alive on the yacht, shouting in berserk rage as they returned fire to the riverboat.

A burst of rounds thwacked into the armored deck on the riverboat. The volley streamed upward and drilled one of the commandos in the shoulder and arm, spinning him around and casting a whirlwind of blood in the air.

A second man on the rifle team was taking aim at the yacht when a burst of autofire scalped him where he stood. He dropped his weapon, his hands clutching at the side rail for a moment before they went deathly still and he dropped flat out onto the deck.

ANTONIO MOURA STAGGERED onto the port side deck, carrying a Heckler & Koch G-3 rifle.

Like a traveler suddenly dropped straight into the heart of Hades, the underground ambassador looked at the volcanic flame that seared the night sky and tried to figure his best way out.

But chaos splintered his thoughts.

Just moments earlier he'd been sleeping the sleep of the just in his cabin, stretched out atop his bed like an emperor on his floating throne.

Then he'd heard the unmistakable chatter of automatic weapons hurling metal rain into the hull. And as the tilting of the yacht spilled him from his sleep, he'd heard the screams of men in mortal fear, the banshee screams of dying beasts.

Moura had swung his legs over the side of the bed, grabbed his weapon and climbed up on deck.

A ribbon of tracer bullets passed over his head, and the crumbling deck shuddered beneath his feet from an explosion in the stern.

The yacht was dying in the water.

The Ambassador crouched low, keeping out of the line of fire from the riverboat that had engaged them in battle. From the dead bodies sprawled around the yacht, most of them men who'd come up from belowdeck as soon as the fighting started, it was obvious that the battle was almost over.

How the hell did it get so close? he thought. What fools let such a ship get within firing range? The questions roared inside his head as the yacht shook again.

But they were questions that couldn't be answered.

More than half of his crew was dead. Of the survivors, another half were wounded, their chorus of bloodcurdling, blood-spilling screams piercing through the menacing clatter of gunfire.

That left only a handful of men alive, and they were frightened out of their wits.

A crewman suddenly appeared in front of Moura. His face was blackened with smoke and grime, and a line of blood streamed down his face.

Moura recognized the wounded man as Luis, a man he knew he could trust when the numbers were with him. But in a tight situation he'd proved to be useless. That was evident from the lack of a weapon in his hand. Luis had thrown down his rifle and was scrambling down the side deck, ready to leap over the side.

"Stop!" Moura shouted, lunging with the Heckler & Koch and gouging the barrel into Luis's chest.

Luis cried out, his eyes seeing demons of battle all around him. It took a moment for him to recognize that the man who'd stopped him was the Ambassador himself, the man whose life he was sworn to protect.

"It's no use," Luis said, shaking his head as he shouted over the din. "We're dead, all dead if we stay on board."

"We're dead if we go into the water," Moura replied. "The current's too strong. We need the Zodiac."

"That's on the other side—"

*"Get it!"* Moura shouted. "Lower it into the water and bring it around here. Or you drag it over here. I don't care how. Just get it."

"It's impossible. I tried to stop them, but there are too many of them. The guns, the grenades..."

"Go," Moura ordered, pushing him backward with the gun barrel.

"I can't."

The Ambassador nodded. He stepped back and lowered the barrel a few inches. Then he pulled the trigger.

The jackhammer burst dropped Luis to his knees, his hands vainly trying to staunch the flow of blood. Then he keeled over onto the deck.

Moura crept close to the wheelhouse and circled around to glimpse the maelstrom.

The Zodiac was almost in reach. But so was the riverboat. He could see the enemy taking careful aim, mechanically chopping down his men. These were professionals, real soldiers. And in that harsh light of battle, Antonio Moura saw the difference between his army and theirs once and for all.

It was the difference between night and day, the difference between life and death.

Forca Militar was going down in flames.

He ran toward the Zodiac, part of his mind thinking he could cut the ropes that moored it to the side. But another part of his mind told him it was impossible.

It didn't matter how slim the chance of escape was. It was all he had left.

He came out firing, unleashing a burst at the riflemen on the upper deck, killing one instantly and causing two others to duck out of sight. He headed for the Zodiac, chanting the word over and over like a man casting his fate. If only he said it long enough he might reach it.

But then he saw one rifleman still standing, a man who didn't fall back from Moura's fire.

The man was tracking him all the way, and Moura knew he wouldn't make it if he kept on the same course.

He turned one more time as he ran across the burning deck with the Heckler & Koch at his hip. He fired a burst and dived into the air, bringing the rifle barrel in front of him as his body made the long arc toward the water.

THE EXECUTIONER STAYED on his man, following his path with the M-16.

The man was diving, diving...dying.

Bolan's full-auto burst stitched Moura from head to toe just as he splashed down into the water.

The corpse was swept away in the currents of darkness...and with it went the black name of Forca Militar.

**18**

*Avenida Rio Branco,*
*Rio de Janeiro*

The first shot of the assault on Castelo dos Machado
began with a television interview.

It was a shot of Colonel Joaquim Almeiros, head of
a special task force combating a subversive underground movement known as Forca Militar.

A statuesque reporter with a telegenic mane of red
hair was interviewing the covert officer for a special
report on the corrupt network of ex-military and intelligence men who made it all possible.

"The rank and file members of the underground
army have been dealt with accordingly," Almeiros
said. "Most of them have been captured or killed in
shootouts with legitimate government forces. These
men were murderers, thieves, brutal dregs of society
who did the dirty work for the secret rulers."

"Who are these secret rulers?"

"Men of power and wealth who hid behind their
positions in the business community."

"Yes," the reporter said. "But are you prepared to name names?"

A pained look appeared on Almeiros's face. "This could be where we lose the war," he said. "Unless the people are behind us, unless they come forward with the details, I'm afraid some of them will remain unknown forever."

"But you said there was an investigation underway."

"There was," Almeiros replied. "But it got stalled along the way—due to influence from high places."

The reporter looked at the camera, a knowing look painted on her face. Scandals in government and industry were nothing new in Brazil. They'd often been uncovered in the past. And just as often they'd been covered up again.

"Do you think you will be able to revive the investigation?"

"We're trying."


"TRY AGAIN, COLONEL," Martin Machado said, using a remote-control unit to turn off the television monitor that was set into a wall unit directly across from his desk. "And maybe someday you can name me." He laughed, his voice echoing across the wide plush suite.

Rather than unsettle him, the report pleased him in a way. It confirmed that the word and wealth of General Machado was still strong enough to buy silence from witnesses who otherwise might have testified against him.

True, Forca Militar was gone. But such organizations could be rebuilt. There were always plenty of men desperate enough to do the dirty work.

In the meantime, he would maintain a low profile.

As long as the others followed suit, they would have nothing to worry about.

Machado picked up the phone from the communications well that was built into the marble-capped desk and called his right-hand man, the former interrogator who'd earned the dreaded name of Inquisitioner. Perhaps Machado should send *him* to speak with the reporter. Maybe some interesting things would turn up.

There was no answer.

That was odd. Like Machado himself, his lieutenant was a creature of habit who often stayed late at the complex while the rest of his civilian workers went to their homes.

He waited a few moments before calling again.

Still no answer.

Machado called security. Two veteran enforcers were always on duty outside the office door.

Always. But not now. No one answered.

He hung up the phone.

Odd, he thought. Too odd.

He headed for the office door.

Halfway there he heard the usual electronic buzz and click as someone from the outside worked the computer-carded lock.

The door swung open and he saw what happened to his guards. Both of them were sprawled on the floor, trails of blood covering the carpet.

And then a man stepped in the doorway, someone dressed entirely in black. A black harness with quick-release Velcro snaps hung from his chest. In the harness was the silenced automatic pistol that had been used on the two gunmen.

The man's face was weathered, bronzed from recent activity in the hot sun of the Amazon, but it was easy to see that he was an American.

It was the American who'd joined forces with Almeiros and helped put Forca Militar out of business.

"Who are you?" Machado asked.

"I think you know that," the Executioner replied. "Just like they do." He jerked his head at the slain security men.

"How did you get in?"

The Executioner shrugged. "Does it matter?"

"Almeiros?"

Bolan nodded. "He's been fighting the war on two fronts. In the Amazon jungle and in the corporate jungle. He's been planning this a long time."

Machado screamed, launching a bizarre tirade that Bolan couldn't completely follow. Nor did he care to. He ignored the verbal barrage and instead kept a hard eye on the little man who'd put a lot of men six feet under. Especially men who underestimated him.

"You're a killer!" Machado gritted.

"When it's called for."

"You're no better than them," Machado said, gesturing at the slain hardmen outside.

"Much better. They're dead. I'm not."

Machado studied the Executioner. And in those eyes he saw a man he couldn't buy. Ever. A man he couldn't frighten. Ever. A man who wouldn't stop coming after him until someone put a bullet in his head.

The Brazilian lunged back toward his desk. He pulled open the top drawer and reached inside for the Hammerli 208 pistol. The engraved and damascened competition weapon held an 8-round clip.

The American stood perfectly still—until Machado brought out the pistol.

Then Bolan's left hand darted to the sound-suppressed automatic, then brought it to bear at the same time as his right hand grabbed the butt of the Model 22. The levering motion triggered the 9 mm weapon and, with a soft cough, a round drilled Martin Machado through the heart.

The war-horse glared at Bolan, then tipped back and dropped behind his desk.

Just as Bolan walked forward to confirm the kill, the telephone began ringing.

The Executioner hesitated for a moment, then picked up the receiver.

"Yeah?"

The voice on the other end of the line was brusque, demanding to talk to Machado. The caller had to warn him about something. "It's urgent," he said. "Let me speak to the general!"

"Sorry," Bolan replied. "The general is retired."

He put down the receiver and walked away.

In the battlefield of covert warfare America's toughest
agents play with lethal precision in the third installment of

# SLAM

## by DAN MATTHEWS

In Book 3: SHADOW WARRIORS, hostile Middle East leaders
are using the drug pipeline to raise cash for a devastating nu-
clear arsenal and the SLAM commando unit is ordered to dismantle the pipeline, piece by piece.

A struggle for survival in
a savage new world.

# JAMES AXLER

# DEATHLANDS®

## Deep Empire

The crystal waters of the Florida Keys have turned into a death
zone. Ryan Cawdor, along with his band of warrior survivalists,
has found a slice of heaven in this ocean hell—or has he?

Welcome to the Deathlands, and the future nobody planned for.

Don't miss out on the action in these titles featuring
**THE EXECUTIONER, ABLE TEAM and PHOENIX FORCE!**